SURE HOPE

—— A NOVEL ——

Jerry A. Miller, Jr.

CAMPEADOR
PRESS

SURE HOPE

Campeador Press

Cover design: Abby Weeks

Author services by Pedernales Publishing, LLC.
www.pedernalespublishing.com

Library of Congress Control Number: 2022916598

ISBN 978-0-9908126-2-3 Paperback Edition
ISBN 978-0-9908126-4-7 Digital Edition

Printed in the United States of America

For my family:
My parents,
My sister,
My wife,
My children,
And my grandchildren—
And for those who came before
And will come after.

… That by two immutable things, in which it was impossible for God to lie,

we might have a strong consolation,

who have fled for refuge to lay hold upon the hope set before us:

Which hope we have as an anchor of the soul, both sure and stedfast…

Hebrews 6:18-19a

CONTENTS

1

A CHRISTMAS PRESENT

Yea, though I walk through the valley
of the shadow of death…

A PETITE YOUNG WOMAN, scarcely nineteen years old, really only a girl, wandered the moonless streets of Sure Hope, Virginia. Over and over, she mumbled some words from Psalm 23, a Psalm she had memorized as a child, but now was unable to remember more than this: *Yea, though I walk through the valley of the shadow of death…* The words seemed appropriate. She had just arrived in Sure Hope after having made the difficult journey by stagecoach from Winchester. She stayed in the shadows of the dark town, hidden and isolated. On her face was her heart, etched with grief, fear, suffering, hopelessness—and love. It was just after 11:00 p.m. on Christmas Eve, 1864. She had a final decision to make and carry out. It would take her the next few hours to decide.

The snow fell wet and heavy from the iron sky. The wind moaned and shrieked from the mountain passes. It was bitterly cold that night in the Shenandoah Valley.

The girl was thin, her body weak, her blue eyes empty, her face gaunt, her skin sallow and pale, her light brown hair without luster. The beauty of her youth had first slowly, then rapidly, vanished. Her threadbare cotton dress and ragged wool shawl did little to keep her warm, yet she shivered without noticing it; her feet were already numb, shod as they were with worn-out shoes wrapped in discarded strips of cloth.

NORTHERN GENERALS DAVID HUNTER and Philip Sheridan, acting on orders from General Ulysses S. Grant, had recently ravaged the Shenandoah Valley during their Valley Campaign of 1864. It was an ugly, evil season of the War Between the States, known as "The Burning." It had been total war, a scorched earth policy, perfected here before General William Sherman later ruthlessly employed it in his March to the Sea. Hunter, Sheridan, and their soldiers had burned homes, barns, crops, and farms. They had stolen and pillaged. They had killed or taken livestock. They had destroyed businesses, shops, and railroads. Hunter had rampaged through Lexington, burning Virginia Military Institute and wrecking Washington College. Even the bedding of innocent women and children had not been spared; it had been shredded. The North had waged war on non-combatants.

The young woman had barely survived the Union terror. She had learned to subsist on the meager rations not destroyed by the Northern soldiers. But the girl had more serious problems. She had lost her father at Gettysburg in 1863, felled by a Union sniper. Her twenty-one-year-old husband, Nathan, also a Confederate soldier fighting to defend his family, had been shot dead at the Battle of Winchester on September 19, 1864. Since her mother had died when the girl was only six years old, and since she was without brothers or sisters, she was alone now. She was a widow and she was an orphan. She was alone. She was without hope and without God in this world—or so she thought.

She now stood in the deep darkness of Sure Hope on Christmas Eve and pressed to her breast a precious bundle, the only thing in all the world of any value to her.

The girl's name was Faith White.

THAT SAME NIGHT, a few hundred yards away, a young couple was preparing for bed. They also carried a deep sadness. They also had endured The Burning and though their home had not been destroyed, the blacksmith husband (whose heavily muscled arms testified to his trade) had lost his forge and tools to the Yankee marauders when they torched and burned his smithy to the ground. The blacksmith was home now only because he had been wounded in battle a few weeks before, a Northern bullet to his right thigh crippling him temporarily. His fight with the Yankees was not to preserve slavery, an institution he abhorred as unspeakably evil; in fact, he had actively worked to destroy it. No, his fight was intensely personal: he fought to protect his home, his family, and his friends.

The couple, as I have said, carried a deep sadness. Their sadness, however, ran deeper than mere material loss, privation, or even the nearness of death.

John and Hannah Soleil had married young. They had begun their lives together loving God, loving each other, and dreaming of having many children. They both loved children. But after three years of marriage, they were childless. Five years went by, and then ten years. Still, no children. The Soleils prayed to God for a baby and they trusted God to give them one. They promised God that they would raise their baby to love the Lord and they earnestly prayed for the child's future service to God. But no baby came. At length, the Soleils learned simply to trust in God's sovereign goodness no matter what happened, resting in his Providence. Realizing that they were not likely to ever have a child, they loved God in the face of sorrow. The sadness of childlessness remained, yet they knew that God understood and stood with them in their disappointment.

This particular Christmas Eve, John and Hannah read the Bible together, re-reading the account of the birth of Christ the Savior. They thanked God for his goodness to the world and to them personally. They kissed each other and went to bed. John drifted to sleep praying for his wife. He loved her and felt her grief at having no children. He knew that she would be such a good mother.

Unusual for her, and without knowing exactly why it occurred just now, Hannah softly wept as she went to sleep that night, crying the tears of a brokenhearted mother who has no children.

Early Christmas morning, John quietly slid out of bed and stepped onto the cold floor. He dressed quickly and added logs to the fire. He recovered the few, simple presents for Hannah that he had hidden and set them out under the Christmas tree. He had cut it down the week before, and he and Hannah together had decorated it with red ribbons and ornaments, saved from the good years before the war. John pulled a chair closer to the fireplace and sat down to drink his coffee as he read his Bible and prayed. Hannah slept a little longer; he was careful not to awaken her.

All was quiet. A fresh blanket of snow covered Sure Hope, muffling all noise. It had snowed the entire night. Suddenly, John heard a knock at the door. Who could that be at six o'clock in the morning? He went to the door and opened it. He looked out, but no one was there, only footprints in the snow. Then he heard a faint noise. What could it be? It was still dark, but he looked down and saw a basket. Had someone left them a Christmas present? Maybe a basket full of fresh bread and homemade jam? Were there Christmas cookies? He grasped the basket by the handle and picked it up; it was heavy. He heard the noise again. He brought the basket inside and as he unwrapped a cloth, something moved: it was not bread and jam. It was a newborn baby. A baby! The baby was well-swaddled and did not appear to be cold. The infant was peering steadfastly and calmly at John. John ran into the bedroom and gently shook Hannah awake. "Hannah, wake up!!"

She could see that John was not himself. "What's wrong?" John was so excited he could barely speak, and what he said made no sense. He simply pointed to the next room, and Hannah got out of bed, wrapped herself in a blanket, and went in. She saw a basket, and in the basket was the most beautiful baby boy she had ever seen. He was alertly gazing at his surroundings with a serious expression on his face. His large head was covered in dark brown hair. His handsome face was pink. His chest was broad. He was a big boy.

Hannah fell to her knees and wept at this boy's

comeliness. She could not help herself as tears of joy and awe flowed in rivulets down her cheeks, the same cheeks that the night before had been stained with tears of disappointment and sadness.

She gently took the boy from the basket, picked him up, held him in her arms and embraced him, rocking him and speaking to him in low, comforting, maternal tones. He continued his steady, calm gaze, never crying.

The Soleils admired the boy in deep wonder for eternal minutes and then realized they did not know where this child had come from. They went to the front door and now, because the snowfall was heavy, any footprints or tracks were quickly disappearing.

They came back inside and inspected the basket for clues. The basket was of straw and revealed nothing. The brown cloth wrapping the boy was actually a piece of a wool blanket. Loosely sewn to the corner of the blanket was a brass button. On the front were the embossed letters CSA. Turning the button over, they noted the initials NW, scratched into the metal with the point of a knife.

John pulled on his coat and boots and limped outside, still moving slowly from his wound. He searched the small town for the next few hours, going from house to house, knocking on doors, questioning neighbors. He was unable to find the bearer of the baby. He thought he discovered a few tracks that led to the banks of the Shenandoah

River, but then they disappeared. Returning home, he told Hannah he was leaving to find the sheriff to report what had happened. The Soleils spent the next few days caring for the baby, and the residents of Sure Hope scoured both the town and the countryside looking for his parents. They searched the nearby woods and they searched up and down the river. No telltale signs were discovered. Neither mother nor father was found. The Soleils waited.

A few weeks later, with no clues at all about the child's identity, John and Hannah adopted the baby boy to be their own son. They named him Beau because, in their eyes, he was the most beautiful boy in the world. They were surprised at how God had answered their prayers for a baby in such an unexpected way. They were thankful. God had given them a son of their own. They loved him, prayed for him, and sang to him. In the years to come, they would teach him about God, the Creator of all, the Sovereign King of the world, the most wonderful and loving Person in the universe.

THEY NEVER DISCOVERED THE mother or father of this precious boy. They assumed that the parents must have been poor and desperate, had heard of the Soleils' deep desire for a baby, and had known they would take care of him. John and Hannah thanked God for the mother of this baby and prayed for her every day. Every year at

Christmas time, they celebrated the birth of Jesus Christ, and they celebrated the birth of their very own Christmas baby, Beau.

AND FAITH WHITE, a girl of whom the world was not worthy, having left her precious bundle on the Soleils' front porch that early Christmas morning, stumbled through a blizzard of snow into the wintry Blue Ridge Mountains, believing she would soon see the face of Christ and join her husband, certain that she had performed her last act of love on this earth. The snowfall eased, then stopped, and the new day broke. The sun slowly dawned, casting its light on the crystal jewels of the snow. And another light arose in Faith's weary heart, enabling her finally to remember the next few words of the verse:

> *Yea, though I walk through the valley*
> *of the shadow of death,*
>
> *I will fear no evil,*
>
> *for Thou art with me.*

2

THE CONVERSATION

THE SOLEIL HOME WAS a world of grace, love, and joy. John led his family with sacrificial love. He worked hard to provide for them and he was alert to protect them. And Hannah was made to be a mother. All of her motherly instincts poured out of her onto and into her new son; she had waited so long for a child of her own. She loved the males in her household in a way only a woman can, with complete support, loyalty, sacrifice, and selflessness. She nurtured Beau and watched him grow. Beau flourished in the rich soil of love, the sunlight of grace, and the water of joy.

Beau was a handsome little boy. His brown hair covered a large head. His brown eyes were so dark they verged on black, and it was difficult to see his pupils except in bright light. He was a big boy and was destined to become a big man.

He developed much as any child would. He walked

and talked at about a year of age. His parents noticed that he was always deeply serious even from a young age. John Soleil often worked hard to get him to laugh. But Beau was serious and introspective from his early years, as if he carried a burden and bore great responsibility. It was not joylessness that made him serious; it was his sense that life was not a game but something to be handled with earnest care. He seemed to know this intuitively from an early age.

Beau loved to play and he loved to think. He stayed outside as long as he could, often doing nothing more than looking at the sky and clouds, observing insects, studying trees and their leaves, or watching the rain and its resulting puddles and torrents. He stepped in every mud puddle he could find.

He had a tender heart. A stern look or impatient word from his father reduced him to tears. He enjoyed going to church and he delighted in hearing Bible stories about God and Jesus. He believed in Jesus as his Savior and loved him for it.

Beau was a gentle little boy. Something inside him told him he was bigger than other children his age, and since he knew his size and strength could hurt others, he had a soft place in his heart for babies and smaller children. He did not want to hurt anyone: he knew he could.

He was also a tough little boy. Beau was able to withstand intense physical pain with little evidence that it bothered him. Part of this had to do with a high pain threshold and part of it had to do with his resolve to not reveal to others when he was hurting. Despite his unusual ability to absorb physical pain, his tender heart made him surprisingly susceptible to deep inner hurt when others wounded him with cruel or even thoughtless, careless words or actions. Yet, he held even these hurts to himself.

John and Hannah noticed that he became angry with others or with himself if he became frustrated. Over the years, the anger became well-corralled and he rarely erupted on others. He learned to use his anger as fuel for accomplishment. He often turned the anger inward onto himself; it seemed safer that way. Beau would deal with this besetting character trait the rest of his life.

The adults surrounding Beau realized he was smart. With the assistance of Hannah, he learned to read by age four. Hannah did not force him to learn; Beau began reading some of the words along with Hannah as she read aloud to him and from there, he progressed to reading himself. Books became a lifelong obsession and he could never read enough. He realized that in books, he could travel anywhere in the world and could meet people who were long dead.

Over time, John and Hannah observed something unusual and worrisome about Beau. He was a fitful sleeper and often, even as a baby, awakened crying and sweating, as if he were having a bad and terrifying dream. They would run to him, pick him up, rock him, speak soft and soothing words to him, and place him back in his crib. "Night terrors," they agreed it had to be. "Lots of children have night terrors. He'll outgrow them," they told each other. Yet he never outgrew them. As he grew older, this pattern continued. The same pattern of crying, sweating, and even screaming would cause his parents to rush into his room in the dark hours of early morning and then gently jostle him and awaken him to say, "Beau, you're dreaming. Wake up!" By the time he was four, Beau was able to describe a dream that kept returning. The basics were always the same but specifics varied. Always, without fail, he saw a sad woman wandering in the dark night in a snowy, shadowy woods. He could not see her face but he knew she was sad. She was slender and her movements seemed aimless. She was carrying a small bundle. And Beau always awakened in sweaty fear and confusion. The recurring dream would plague him for years.

BEAU GREW AND HE flourished. He spent hours with his father in the blacksmith shop and learned early how to wield a hammer and drive a nail. As his father worked, he talked with Beau. He taught him about life and people and nature. The two were constant companions.

Hannah Soleil provided the nurture and encouragement for Beau that only a mother can. She understood him. She could see the inner conflicts he had with situations and himself. She bandaged his scrapes and wounds. Her hugs and words were salve for his inner wounds as well. Hannah accepted her son as a gift, and she loved him in such a way that he could never think otherwise.

Soon after supper each night, Beau began his bedtime routine. His parents usually read to him and then moved to the bedroom. There, John read a few verses of Scripture to him and all three of them kneeled to pray together. They tucked Beau into bed and kissed him. John and Beau often spent a few more moments together before he blew the candle out. Often, John lay down beside Beau in his bed and they talked. John taught him a memory game using his five fingers. "Beau, hold up your hand like this," John said. "Look at my hand. Do you see my five fingers? Here is what they stand for. Wise, strong, kind, brave, true. Five fingers. Five words." They counted down the fingers with the words attached to each one so many times that Beau never forgot this was the man John Soleil wanted him to become.

Before he went to sleep himself, John Soleil secured the house, checked the fire, and blew out all the candles. And more often than not, he crept into Beau's room and dropped to his knees beside Beau's bed. He placed his strong, gentle hand on Beau's sleeping head and prayed. "O God, thank you for this boy. Keep him safe tonight. Bless him as he grows. Make him a man who loves you and loves others."

BEAU SOLEIL TURNED six years old in 1870. Since his actual birthdate was not certain, John and Hannah marked and celebrated Beau's birthday every Christmas Day, the day he was given to them. Beau opened a few simple presents including a new winter coat and a new shirt. The best present of all was a new pocketknife forged with love by John Soleil. There were advantages to having a blacksmith for a father. Hannah made Beau a birthday cake and, as friends and family watched, Beau blew out all six lighted candles with one breath. He was growing quickly now.

John and Hannah always knew that at some time they would need to have a conversation with Beau. He needed to know he had been adopted and he needed to know it from them.

After the double celebration of the birth of Christ and then of Beau, and after all the gathered friends and relatives had gone home, Beau prepared for bed. He had his new knife with him as he crawled under the covers. His father had already sternly, lovingly warned him, "Beau, be careful with it. The knife is sharp and it is not a toy. It is a tool and a weapon. I think you're old enough to handle it. I do not want you playing with it or cutting yourself with it." Beau took his father's words to heart.

Both John and Hannah walked into Beau's room. Hannah sat on the edge of his bed and John pulled up a chair to be close.

John started to talk. "Beau, happy birthday. You are a fine son and we love you. We are proud of you and we are so grateful to God for you. Have you had a good time today?"

"Oh, Daddy and Mama, this has been the best day of my life. Thank you for a great day and for my presents. Especially the knife!" Beau grinned, revealing the gaps left by the few baby teeth that had fallen out, as he pulled the knife from beneath his blanket. He would sleep with that knife each night for a long time.

"Beau, we want to talk to you about something important." John seemed reluctant to go on.

Beau sensed that something serious was coming and he waited.

"Beau, six years ago on Christmas Day, I got up early like I always do. At about six o'clock, I heard a knock at the front door. When I opened the door, no one was there. But there was a basket on the porch. And in that basket was a baby." John stopped the story to allow Beau time to take it in.

"Go on, Daddy," Beau encouraged.

"Well, Beau, I took the basket and the baby inside.

The baby was a boy. Your mother and I thought he was the most beautiful baby in the world. He was. We searched for the baby's mother and father and we could never find them. We took that baby into our home and we adopted him to be our son. That baby boy, Beau, was you." John stopped here and his eyes and Hannah's were tearing up.

"Beau, God gave us a son that day. He chose you for us and he gave you to us. You have been the biggest gift we have ever known besides God himself and each other." John went on to explain some of the specifics of the search and of the next few days after Beau had been given to them.

A shadow passed over Beau's face and he became serious and grave. He lay in his bed quietly and thoughtfully for a few moments, looking at his parents. He had some questions.

"Mama, you mean I was not born to you?"

"That's right, Beau," Hannah gently answered.

"And my mother knocked on your door and then left me on your porch? Why would she do that? Didn't she love me?"

"Beau, your mother left you on our porch because she thought it best and safest for you. She knew we would find you right away, and we did. Your mother did not desert you. I became your mother that day and have been ever since. I love you as much or more than if I had given birth to you myself. We know nothing about your mother who gave you birth. But I am certain she loved you. I think that's why she left you for us to care for. At the end of the war, times were hard. Many men had been killed. These men were fathers, husbands, sons, and brothers. The war created many young widows and orphans. Food was hard to come by. It was not easy to earn a living. Confederate money was worthless.

"I think probably your mother placed you on our porch because she was one of those young women whose lives had been destroyed by the war. She had a new baby and she knew she could not afford to feed or care for him. She may have been dying herself. She did not *want* to leave you. She loved you so much she *had* to leave you for someone else to care for. She wanted you to live, even if she died. She wanted you to live even if it meant she had to give her precious newborn son to someone else to care for and love. Can you imagine how hard her decision was? She must have felt like she was dying inside. No, Beau, your mother loved you very much. I think that's why she left you for us to take care of. It was not because she did not love you. It was because she loved you so much. And we love you very much."

Hannah allowed Beau to think about all of this for a few minutes. Hannah could see the serious, confused, thoughtful look on his face. She and John had prayed much about this talk. They wanted to be honest with Beau and also to be sure he knew how loved and secure he was. John and Hannah had been dreading this conversation.

After a few minutes, Hannah continued. "So you see, Beau, your mother loved you. She did the best thing for you she could think of. She gave you to someone who would be able to take care of you. She gave you to us. God gave you to us. God chose you and he chose us to come together as a family. And we are so glad you are ours. You are our son, our only son, and we love you. We could not possibly love you more if I had given birth to you. Your mother could not possibly love you more than to have placed you where you could be well cared for; it was for your good. She did what she thought was best. And God could not possibly love you more than he does."

Beau silently pondered all of this new information. His mind was a storm of confusion, doubts, questions, and surprises. He did not say anything for a few minutes as he tried mightily to make sense of this news. He ordered his thoughts the best he could. He finally spoke.

"Daddy and Mama, this is a big surprise to me. I love you both. You are good parents and you have loved me and taken care of me. I love my mother for loving me so much that she would give me to someone else because she couldn't take care of me. And I love God for giving me to you."

Beau's mature words showed his love, his gratitude, and his unwillingness to hurt his parents by saying anything that might cause them distress. After all, they had adopted him and loved him: they had taken in an orphan.

Yet, this would not be the end of his questions. Over the ensuing years, he would need to revisit this conversation with his parents many times as he sorted through his many conflicting thoughts and doubts. They would talk openly and freely and honestly. Beau would come away from each discussion reassured of the love of God, the love of his parents, and the love of an unknown mother who would sacrifice herself that her son might live. And he kept an unspoken thought to himself: he wondered what had become of his mother that cold winter night in 1864.

Now, the three Soleils hugged and kissed each other as they cried joyful tears.

Hannah had a small object in her hand. She now opened her hand and placed it in Beau's.

"Beau, here is something we think is important for you to have. When your mother delivered you to us early that Christmas morning, you were wrapped in a little blanket. This was sewn to the corner. We have kept it for you until this moment. We do not know what it means, but you may discover its meaning someday. I hope it will remind you of the love of your mother and the love of God."

Beau took the last gift of Christmas and his birthday from his mother and gazed at it. It was a little brass button, somewhat tarnished, with the raised letters CSA on the front. Rolling it over in his hands, he noticed something had been scratched on the back, the letters NW.

What did it all mean? Beau was not sure. He did know he would cherish this button all his life as a symbol of love: the love of his mother, the love of his adoptive father and mother, and the love of God.

Beau kept that button his entire life. As he grew older, he always had it in the left pocket of his trousers, ready for him to touch at all times. He found himself reaching for it to roll in his fingers especially in times of deep thought or anxiety. The button somehow made him feel better and helped him to think more clearly. It somehow provided him comfort. The button lost its tarnish as he kept it with him and handled it. It became bright and shiny.

That night, the dream returned, and in the dream, the sad, slender, enigmatic woman who wandered in the snow.

And the shiny, mysterious brass button in his pocket became Beau Soleil's constant, lifelong reminder that he was loved. The button was a token that anchored him to reality, the true reality that is beneath and in every truth in the universe: the love of God.

3

SUMMER

SUMMERTIME IN SURE HOPE was pure pleasure for a six-year-old boy.

Each morning, Beau got up early, just as the sun stole over the mountain and shone through the white cotton curtains of his east-facing room. He leapt out of bed, ready for a new day, ready for new adventures, and most of all ready for breakfast. His mother prepared eggs and biscuits for him almost every morning. Beau attacked his breakfast with hungry gusto and washed it down with a glass of milk from their neighbor's cow. The biscuits were his favorite part of breakfast. He made certain that they were dripping with plenty of butter and blackberry jam. After he finished, his mother wiped the blackberry jam from his face. There was no immediate remedy for what he dropped onto his shirt.

Then he went about his work for the day. He played in the woods, fragrant with the aroma of damp earth, sweet mountain grass, and honeysuckle, the sun's rays shooting like arrows between the branches of firs and hardwoods. He went to the shore of the Shenandoah River to collect frogs and bugs. He was allowed to play on the riverbank, but could not get near the water unless his father was with him. He dug in the dirt and mud; he made castles and houses. He put shiny, sparkling rocks in his pockets. He fished when his father went with him, and when they got hot, they jumped into the river to cool off.

He returned home for lunch, and afterwards, his mother made him rest. Not that he was ever tired, of course, but somehow he always wound up going to sleep. He always said that he never slept—he was only resting his eyes, he said, and was wide awake the whole time he was in bed. After his nap, he refueled on milk and bread, always with butter and blackberry jam. He went back to work until dinnertime.

At night, he chased lightning bugs darting around the backyard and hiding in the mimosa trees. When he caught them, he carefully placed them in a glass jar to light his way. In the dark skies surrounding Sure Hope, he saw shooting stars. His father taught him to recognize the constellations of the summer night sky. Beau learned where to look for the Big Dipper, Orion, the North Star, and the Evening Star.

It was a good life for a little boy. No—it was better. It was Paradise.

ONE WEEK EACH SUMMER, Sure Hope Presbyterian Church had a special week for the children of the church and town. Of course, it was known as Children's Week. Beau and the other children looked forward to this week with eagerness.

The children went to the church each morning and spent the time learning about Jesus and the Bible, singing, and creating things out of paper and paste. They had cookies and sliced fruit at break time. They went out to play games or just run around on the church lawn. This was Beau's second year to attend. He was excited about it and he loved it. His teacher for the week was Mrs. LeBlanc.

Beau was the youngest boy there, and his neighbor, sweet little Grace McLeod, was the youngest girl. Grace was only five years old. She was petite (and would stay petite all her life) but her size belied her power. She was a girl to be dealt with.

Grace had a deep, sensitive, loving heart. She was full of intense emotion. Grace knew what she liked and what she did not like. She knew whom she liked and whom she did not like. She had a deep sense of truth and justice. Grace's love burned and her anger raged with equal intensity. Her fierce loyalty knew no limits. Grace had no guile. She was an open book.

Grace's steady brown eyes could peer into situations and into souls. Without meaning to and without even knowing it, Grace made you feel as if you could not hide anything from her, that you did not *want* to hide anything from her, that you must be as honest with her as she was with you. Her brown hair lay in ringlets around her expressive, beautiful oval face. Her skin was fair and Celtic.

Grace's honesty and intensity both allowed and caused her to sleep well every night—her honesty provided her with a clear conscience and her intensity exhausted her. She could sleep well anywhere and almost at any time when given the opportunity. She often fell asleep at the dinner table and her father would then carry her into her bedroom for a night of peaceful slumber.

Grace's amazing propensity for sleeping occasionally caused some problems. Once, her parents realized that Grace was missing. They called her name. They frantically searched the house and the nearby woods. No Grace. Mr. McLeod mounted his horse and called on all the neighbors to ask if she were there or if they had seen her. No Grace.

Finally, just as they began to panic, her parents remembered that Grace loved to crawl into a small closet beneath the stairs in their home. Light filtered through the cracks in the stairway planking. This vestibule was her hiding place of choice. The McLeods opened the door to the closet and there was Grace, sound asleep with her favorite picture book by her side.

Grace had a younger sister named Martha who was

four years old. She also had a younger brother, David, who was two. From his birth, David had not been normal. He could not communicate verbally except in grunts and groans and moans. He could not walk because his arms and legs were rigid and contracted; they could not be extended. He had great difficulty swallowing and eating. David was a source of great joy and of great sadness to the McLeods. Grace loved this little boy and helped her mother care for him with painstaking attention. David and Grace understood each other, and Grace's heart was always tender toward her disabled little brother. Grace spoke softly and gently to him and he answered with his eyes and with moans whose different pitches meant different things; Grace could interpret them all. Grace often rocked her little brother and sang to him. David shaped Grace's view of the world. And David knew Grace loved him.

The Soleils and the McLeods were friends. This meant that Beau and Grace also were friends and they played together often. Beau was usually considerate of Grace. The year before, Grace had been sick and had not been able to attend Children's Week. So each day on the way home, Beau had gone to Grace's house to deliver a few crumbling cookies he had saved for her. He carried the cookies, wrapped in a napkin that he clutched in his sweaty hands, all the way to her home. He told her about all the fun they were having.

Sometimes Beau showed his affection for Grace by tossing pebbles at her or by teasing her. Boys can have strange ways of showing that they care.

And to Grace, Beau was about the best boy in the whole world.

THE OLDER CHILDREN were kind to the younger ones and tried to take care of them. That is, everyone but nine-year-old Rufus Crabtree. Rufus was a bully and a blowhard. He was a big kid who was used to getting his way. He was sneaky. He was loud and he was crude. He also smelled bad. No one really liked him, but most of the other kids were afraid of him, and they did pretty much what he wanted them to. If not, he would pitch a fit, get red in the face, yell, and hit something—or *someone.*

Rufus had never received enough spankings.

On Wednesday of Children's Week, Rufus became angry at eight-year-old Wesley Threlkeld, Beau's best friend. Mrs. LeBlanc had just commented on what a beautiful drawing Wes had made. Wes had also recited his Bible memory verses perfectly that day. Rufus felt disrespected because no one had singled him out for praise all week. It hurt his feelings. He decided to make Wes pay. At break time, out on the church lawn, he walked up to Wes and glared at him. "Wes, I think your drawing was terrible."

"Aw, you're just jealous," Wes said.

Rufus was surprised Wes had responded like that. Nobody ever talked to Rufus Crabtree like that. "Who're you calling jealous?"

"Who do you think, you big bully?"

Rufus's face got red. His veins popped out on his neck. He was getting really mad. And this was just the chance he was hoping for "Take it back, Wes! Take it back!"

"I won't take it back!" Wes said. He stood his ground. "What I said is true. You are a big, jealous bully! Go ahead, do something about it! You wanna fight about it?" Wes knew he was safe here. He knew Rufus would never start a fight at church.

But where Wes saw safety, Rufus saw opportunity. He had planned this perfectly. And Wes had underestimated Rufus's jealousy. Rufus ran at Wes and knocked him down, then began to pummel him with his fists. All the kids gathered around them and watched the fight, cheering for Wes. Mrs. LeBlanc, inside the church arranging the snacks, heard the commotion and ran outside. She was 67 years old, 4'11", and weighed 97 pounds (with her shoes on). But she was a human ball of energy, and all the boys feared her. She grabbed Rufus by the collar and dragged him off of Wes. Both boys were dirty and sweaty. Wes had a bloody nose, and they both had blood all over their shirts. But Rufus wasn't hurt. That did not stop him from playing this event to his own advantage and to the hilt. He got up quickly and began to cry—no, he began to wail, and huge tears began to roll down his cheeks. He was a good actor. Wes got up and said not a word. Wes was bound by the honor code of boys not to snitch on another boy, even if the other boy was a rat. But not Rufus. No—not Rufus. He began to whine as he sobbed and blubbered, "Wes started it! He called me names, and he asked me if I wanted to fight about it! He jumped on me and started to hit me. He made me fight him. I was only trying to tell him how good his picture was! He made fun of mine!"

As Mrs. LeBlanc looked from boy to boy, Rufus glowered at Wes as if to say, "Keep your mouth shut. Don't say a word to get me in trouble—or you'll pay!"

Mrs. LeBlanc asked Wes what had happened, and he didn't say anything, not out of fear but out of honor. Rufus, however, filled the void, jumped right in, and kept up his accusations. The little human dynamo sensed that something was amiss, and she intuitively did not trust Rufus. But since his was the only side of the story to come out, she decided she had to punish both boys for fighting. They could not come back on Thursday, and would be allowed back Friday only if they said they were sorry to each other.

Friday, the last day of Children's Week, arrived and both Rufus and Wes came to the church. Rufus made a big show of apologizing to Wes. "I'm sorry that you took what I said in the wrong way. I'm sorry you get your feelings hurt so easily. Let's be friends." He stuck out his big, chubby hand in friendship. As I said, he was a good actor.

Wes mumbled that he was sorry, but inside, he was not sorry one bit except for one thing—he was sorry he had not clobbered Rufus.

Mrs. LeBlanc thought that was the best they could do for now, and so let them both return.

NOW RUFUS HAD MADE fun of Beau all week. He made fun of his name, he laughed at his singing, he mocked his artwork. And all the other kids laughed, too, when Rufus told them to. Except for Wes, no one would stand up to Rufus. The taunting made Beau feel bad. He went home crying twice that week.

Rufus's day off on Thursday for misbehavior had not gone to waste. He told his mother he was sick and stayed in bed until after lunch. His mother had no reason to believe her beloved little boy had done anything wrong. Rufus spent the day thinking and plotting. After all, he was a natural-born genius. He had an inspiration. He would finish the week with his best, meanest trick ever. The church had a storage building on the edge of its property, and Rufus gathered two of his fearful friends to help him. He made them promise to keep a secret. He told them he would beat them up if they ever let even a word of the plan slip out. They promised to keep their mouths shut.

Just after Friday's last session was over and hours after Rufus had made his pseudo-apology, all the singing done and all the artwork cleaned up, the children were leaving. As Beau left, Rufus called to him. "Beau, come over here. I want to show you something." He lured him over to the storage building where his two comrades were waiting. "Beau," they called, "c'mere. Look at this!" Beau couldn't resist his curiosity. He knew he shouldn't trust Rufus, but he was being nice to him now, and the two friends, Jack Aranda and Tommy Marcoux, had always been kind to him. So he went with Rufus and walked to the storage building.

Once there, all four boys looked into the building through the dirty nine-pane window in the door. It was dark inside. "I can't see anything," said Beau. "Look harder!" Rufus said. "Here, let me lift you up so you can see better."

Rufus lifted Beau, and at the same time the other boys opened the door. Rufus carried Beau into the building, threw him onto the floor, rushed out, and slammed the door. The boys held the door closed as Rufus pulled a lock from his pocket and locked Beau in. Rufus stood there, dangling the key in his hand, laughing at Beau.

Beau was afraid. He was locked in. He stood there crying as he looked through the window at his laughing tormentors. His own thoughts began to terrify him. "What if I can't get out? What if they leave me here? What if no one knows I'm here? What if no one misses me? What if there are snakes in this dark shed?"

Then he began to get angry. What had he ever done to these boys to deserve this? His child's sense of justice told him this was wrong. His only offense was that he was smaller and younger than they were.

The more Beau cried, the more Rufus laughed at him, and the more frightened and angry Beau became. His fear and rage controlled him now. Jack and Tommy gradually realized they were doing something very wrong. "C'mon, Rufus. Let him out! You've had your fun. He's scared. Let him out!"

"Never!" replied Rufus. He was laughing so hard he could barely speak. Cruelty can have strange manifestations. He would not let him go.

Beau realized there was only one thing left to do. He could think of only one thing. He must get out, no matter what. And he did what he had to do.

He made a fist with his right hand and he punched it through one of the lower panes of glass. He reached for the key dangling in Rufus's hand and grabbed for it without success. Now it was Rufus's turn to be afraid. Beau's hand was streaming blood. The smashed pane had made a shattering noise that echoed all over the churchyard. And the three boys were caught in the middle of their crime when Mrs. LeBlanc came flying out of the church. Little Grace McLeod was right behind her, trying to keep up, running as fast as her legs would take her.

Rufus was afraid now that he was caught. Jack and Tommy were afraid that Beau might bleed to death. They quickly snatched the key from Rufus and unlocked the door. Beau came running out with hot tears of anger on his cheeks. Blood was on his right hand and shirt, but he didn't even realize that he was hurt.

Mrs. LeBlanc ran to Beau and looked at his hand. Her eyes filled with tears of compassion and anger. By then, strong and gentle Grace McLeod had caught up and was beside the teacher. Grace was crying with fear, love, and wrath—mainly wrath—as she looked softly at Beau saying, "Oh, Beau, are you hurt badly?" and then glared with fiery rage at the other boys and screamed, "You boys are so mean!!"

With a clean towel, Mrs. LeBlanc bandaged Beau's hand. At the same time, she commanded the big boys to stay where they were. "Don't move! Stay right where you are!" They cowered and they obeyed the little woman. She knew exactly what had happened.

As she wrapped Beau's hand, she was surprised that he had sustained only some scratches. There were no deep wounds, and the bleeding stopped quickly. She silently thanked God for protecting him; she believed in guardian angels.

She turned to the criminals. "Boys, do you realize what you have done? Beau could have been badly hurt, or he could have died. How would that have made you feel?" Rufus was feeling bad that he had been caught. Jack and Tommy were truly sorry for what they had done and said so to Beau.

Rufus was really only sorry for himself. He knew he just might be in trouble. He felt no remorse, only a little regret, and saw no need to apologize to Beau.

Mrs. LeBlanc told the three delinquents to go home and tell their parents what they had done, fully expecting their parents to contact her and let her know what their discipline would be. She walked Beau home herself and explained to the Soleils what had happened. Beau's parents were furious, especially his father. John Soleil was not someone you wanted mad at you. He was an otherwise kind, gentle man but his anger was like a volcano if someone hurt his family, and he was erupting now. Hannah Soleil tried to calm her husband. John vowed that he would see justice done. In his fury, he went to his forge, picked up his hammer, and beat mercilessly on the horseshoes he was making. He had learned many years before to let his anger cool before he acted, and the best way to cool off was in his hot forge, hammering some piece of metal into submission. He worked and he thought.

The Soleils had visitors that night. Jack Aranda, Tommy Marcoux, and their fathers all came to the Soleils' home. The boys again asked for Beau's forgiveness and told him this type of thing would never happen again. Jack and Tommy received a gift from their fathers to help them remember to keep their promise: two weeks of hard farm labor.

Rufus Crabtree never came by, nor did his father. Still seething, but controlled, John Soleil went to the Crabtree home after a day of silence and explained to the Crabtrees what had happened. Not surprisingly, Rufus had not told them. Mr. Crabtree's initial response was involuntary, nervous laughter. He didn't know what to do with his son. He had never disciplined him, but had let him have his own way. He believed that his son must find his own path to goodness. Obviously, the plan had not worked very well. Mr. Crabtree offered a sincere apology for his son's behavior because he really was sorry for what had happened. He was also a little worried that the blacksmith might do something violent—a blacksmith's arms can do some harm. Rufus stayed in the corner of the room and never uttered a word until his father begged him, "Rufus, did you make a wise decision? Won't you please, please tell Mr. Soleil you are sorry? If you do, I'll have your mother make you a special dessert tonight."

After Rufus negotiated for apple pie, he did his best to appear penitent and muttered, "I'm sorry, Mr. Soleil."

Spineless Mr. Crabtree turned to his son and said, "Rufus, thank you so much for doing the right thing. You're a special person." He apologized again to Mr. Soleil with a look on his face as if to say that was all he could do.

These proceedings gave Beau's father no satisfaction at all. He looked both Crabtree males in their eyes and told them that his son must never be bullied again by Rufus—not ever—not even once. He made it clear to them that he would hold them both responsible. John Soleil was not a man to be crossed when it came to his family, and even Rufus felt the chill. Mr. Crabtree almost threw up. Rufus almost wet his pants. Mr. Soleil left angrily. Rufus gorged away his guilt on apple pie that night.

WHEN SCHOOL BEGAN a few weeks later, Rufus bragged about his best dirty trick ever, the locking away of Beau. The other children despised him for it and grew tired of hearing about it. Rufus continued to tease and bully the little children and it was now worse than ever. Everyone decided that someone needed to teach Rufus a lesson. But no one did anything. Living in fear is a bad way to live. Wes Threlkeld just listened. He kept quiet. He waited. He bided his time. And then he determined it was time to put Rufus in his place. The children could not be bullied forever.

It was time for the day of reckoning. Judgment day was nigh.

After school one day, Wes approached Rufus and before he could say anything, Rufus said, "Well, what have we here? It's the village idiot!" Rufus was always saying nice things like that.

"Rufus," Wes said, "you owe someone an apology."

"Aww, did I hurt little Wes's feelings? Does he need for me to say I'm sorry?"

"I'm not talking about me, Rufus. What you did to Beau a few weeks ago was mean and hateful. You're a bully. You're a coward. And you run around bragging about it like you're some kind of evil genius. You need to tell him you are sorry, and you need to shut your mouth about it after that."

"And who can make me do it? You? Aren't you the boy I just beat up a few weeks ago? Go ahead, do something about it. Make me. You want to fight about it?"

Here, Wes knew he had reached the decision point. He could either yield to his fear or he could do the right thing, no matter what it cost him. He was not going to back down now. He had also learned from the last fight that after a certain amount of talking, you had to quit the talk and start the action.

"No, Rufus, I don't want to fight." He turned as if to go, and Rufus was feeling good about winning another battle by just being a bully.

Rufus yelled at Wes, "Hey Wes, turn around and fight! What's wrong, are you scared?"

Wes replied, still with his back toward Rufus, "No, I'm not afraid of you. And no, I don't want to fight you, Rufus. I don't *want* to fight. But you're making me." And then, suddenly and with one motion, Wes wheeled around, pivoting on his right foot, leaning forward to shift his weight to his left, and drove his right fist into Rufus's doughy belly. Rufus bent over in pain, and as he did, Wes followed that blow with a left uppercut to Rufus's chin. Rufus crumpled to the ground. His chin was bleeding. He was crying like a little girl.

"Get up, Rufus! Get up!" Wes was standing over him like a lion rampant. "I'm not done yet! You need a lesson in manners. Get up! I'm going to hit you again!"

Rufus lay on the ground, whimpering like a whipped puppy. He cried and he howled. He would not get up. The other kids circled the two boys and watched in a strange mixture of horror and satisfaction. One of the girls had some of Rufus's blood spattered on her dress. Fights are never pretty.

"Wes, if I get up, will you promise not to hit me again? I promise I'll never be a bully again. I promise I'll ask Beau's forgiveness."

Wes unclenched his fists. It was over. He reached for Rufus's hand and helped him get up.

As Rufus slowly rose, he stooped in a crouch as if he were in pain. Then he lunged at Wes to tackle him. Rufus was being Rufus again. He made a slight miscalculation, however. He rammed his nose into Wes's knee. He knocked himself out, and his nose was streaming blood. He came to a few minutes later, still woozy. He got up, and this time Wes had his fists ready. But Rufus was defeated. He had no desire for more punishment. He was a mess. Blood was all over his face and clothes, mixed with dirt and sweat. It was over. Really over.

"Please don't hit me again, Wes!" Rufus gasped between sobs. "You win. I'm sorry for picking a fight with you a few weeks ago." He turned to Beau, who had just arrived at the outer edge of the circle. "Beau, what I did to you was wrong. I am sorry. Please forgive me."

Beau was still afraid of Rufus, and he still did not trust him. But Rufus seemed sincere, and Beau told him he forgave him.

Rufus Crabtree never bullied anyone again. Frontier justice had had its desired effect, and Rufus was on his way to becoming a different person.

Every dog has his day.

Evil always overplays its hand.

And sometimes you have to fight for what is right.

4

BEAU SOLEIL GETS A CHRISTMAS PRESENT

SEVEN-YEAR-OLD Beau Soleil enjoyed school (most of the time) and was a good student. He was one of the smartest boys in the small school. He worked hard, he studied hard, and his grades were always near the top of the class. His teacher was a nice lady named Mrs. Huffnagle. She was strict but fair. The children liked her because she was even, not at all moody, and they knew what to expect from her. In addition, her students knew what she expected from them. She would not put up with misbehavior, but she created an atmosphere of joy in her classroom. Knowing what to expect, knowing what the rules were, and knowing they would be applied fairly helped the children to enjoy her teaching and to thrive.

On December 15th, Mrs. Huffnagle began the day as she always did. She asked one of the children to read a passage from the Bible. Then they all said the Lord's Prayer together.

Afterwards, Mrs. Huffnagle cleared her throat and said, "Children, before we begin our work today, I have a very special announcement. I have in my hand a letter from Mr. James Argenta, our former mayor and one of the leading men of Sure Hope. He and his wife have invited all the children in town to their home for their annual Christmas party next Wednesday. He hopes all of you can come." Mrs. Huffnagle paused for a few seconds to listen to the children laugh and giggle about the party. They remembered how wonderful these parties were. They knew that Mr. Argenta was not only a leader, but he was the richest man in town. He had become rich by working hard and running businesses. He was also a Christian, and because of that he was generous. He helped other people. His businesses provided needed jobs. He often helped the poor, widows, and orphans by paying for their food, clothing, or medicine; he usually made the gifts without anyone knowing he was doing it. And sometimes, like a magician, he made money appear at the homes of certain families in need. Where it came from, the families did not know, but it often caused them to thank God for the gift.

In 1872, Sure Hope was a poor town. It was still recovering from the War Between the States. Money was scarce. Most of the men were veterans of the war, many of them with amputations or other permanent injuries. They worked mainly as farmers or coal miners. It was hard and dangerous work that provided little margin if someone became ill or injured. Some of the men worked in businesses started by Mr. Argenta. But often, many families of Sure Hope had barely enough to eat. The children were excited to be invited to a nice party given by Mr. Argenta.

As the time for the party drew near, the children became more and more excited. Finally, Wednesday arrived. Right after school, the children would all go over to Mr. Argenta's home. They all wore their best clothes to school.

The day seemed to last forever, but finally Mrs. Huffnagle rang the school bell at three o'clock and the children gave a huge cheer. They were excited about Christmas, about getting out of school for Christmas vacation, and about the big party. They were almost uncontrollable.

They lined up as Mrs. Huffnagle gave them instructions and walked, hopped, and skipped to Mr. Argenta's home. As they arrived, it began to snow. The flakes were big and wet and heavy. Some of the children caught snowflakes on their tongues.

They went inside the front gate, and Beau was again surprised, as he always was, at the size of the house. He had forgotten how big the Argenta home was. There were gigantic oak trees in the front yard. The two-story red brick house had four white columns in front. On the front door, hanging on a brass knocker, was a cedar wreath bedecked with a red bow.

Mrs. Huffnagle knocked on the door. Within a few seconds, a smiling Mrs. Argenta opened it and let them in. Mrs. Argenta was wearing a white apron over her red Christmas dress and she gave them a hearty welcome: "Merry Christmas, children!" She invited them to help themselves to the table laden with punch and hot chocolate and Christmas cookies. The Argentas had a ten-foot Christmas tree just beside the stairway, and it was decorated with strands of cranberries and popcorn, along with shiny gold and silver ornaments hanging from the branches. Beau loved the way the tree smelled, freshly cut and dragged from the woods; the scent of pine wafted through the air. The fireplace contained a roaring fire, and blazing oak logs popped and cracked. Mr. Argenta moved to the fireplace to add another log to the fire as Beau headed toward it to warm his hands. In the corner of the great living room, some of the children began to sing Christmas carols as the town music teacher, Mrs. Melisma, played the piano for them. Beau ate a few of Mrs. Argenta's famous Christmas cookies, the kind with red and green sugar sprinkles on top of white icing, the kind with raisins on the inside, the kind that crunch when you chew them, the kind that dissolve in your mouth as soon as you crunch them. Oh yes, this was a good party.

JUST THEN, BEAU HEARD a loud cry for help, and all the music stopped. All eyes were on a little blond-headed boy in the corner of the dining room. He had a cookie in one hand, crumbs on his face, a milk mustache, and an arm caught in the chair he was sitting in. It was Mr. Argenta's four-year-old grandson, Charlie. Charlie had somehow managed to wedge his left arm between the pickets in the chair-back, and now it was stuck. He tried to be brave, but it was clear that he was scared and he fought back tears. It only hurt when he tried to pull his arm out. Mr. James Argenta walked quickly to his grandson and calmed him. James Argenta was a big man with a poorly managed shock of graying blond hair. He was tall and muscular and broad-chested. He was not the kind of man you would want to fight. But his eyes were blue and gentle, and they were often moist from love, sympathy, or joy. Mr. Argenta was a teddy-bear of a man. He was strong and he was gentle. He smiled at Charlie and tried to free his arm. It would not come out. "Charlie," he said, "somehow you got your arm stuck, and so I'm sure we can get it out!" He worked with him some more and still couldn't free him. "Charlie, maybe you'll have to carry this chair around with you the rest of your life," he joked to his grandson, trying to make him smile and distract him. Charlie was crying and panicking now; his arm still would not budge. Mr. Argenta began to worry a little and wondered if he should get his saw and cut the back of the chair to free Charlie. Suddenly, he knew what he should do. He asked his wife to bring some lard from the kitchen and then he coated Charlie's arm with it. With a gentle and steady pull, he was able to slip his arm free. Everyone cheered and Charlie hugged his grandfather. The crisis was over.

THE HOUSE AGAIN WAS full of laughter and fun almost immediately after this little emergency. About half an hour later, Mrs. Argenta announced that there was a present for every child there. Just then, Mr. Argenta appeared from the kitchen, went to the dining room, and took off the tablecloth that was covering what had appeared to be a mound of boxes. There, on the table, were dozens of wrapped presents for the children. Mr. Argenta invited each child to come up and receive a gift. Each boy got a shiny toy train engine and each girl got a new doll. The children all thanked Mr. and Mrs. Argenta. They were thrilled because most of the children were poor and expected very little from their parents for Christmas. Beau also knew that his parents would be unable to give him much for Christmas.

Everyone stayed and played for another hour or so.

Then Mr. Argenta tapped on a glass with a spoon, creating a tinkling sound to get their attention. It was now about five o'clock. It was starting to get dark and it was snowing heavily. He wanted all the boys and girls to make it home safely, so he said it was about time to leave. He told them he had one more gift for each of them. "Children," he said, "Mrs. Argenta and my five daughters have been making special homemade bread for the past two days. We want each of you to have a loaf to take home for your families to enjoy." At that, the children lined up again, but this time they were not as patient or orderly as they had been. The delightful smell of the warm, freshly baked bread drew them to another table that had been set up in the living room. On this table there was a mountain of bread, stacked neatly like bricks, and they could not resist the aroma or the thought of having the bread for dinner that night. Many of the children rushed the table, pushing to get a loaf, while a few waited patiently until it was their turn. In all the commotion and jostling, Beau wound up in the back of the line. He was not willing to push and shove. Was it because of selflessness? Or did he have great self-control? Or was he ashamed to think he would fight for a loaf of bread? Whatever the reason, he stayed back and arrived at the table last. Dead last. Almost there, he saw that there were only five loaves left and each one was the same size except for one, which was only about half the size of all the others. He finally got to the table to see that the children in front of him had taken all the larger loaves, leaving only one loaf for him. It was the little one. He picked it up and was silently disappointed. He did not show what he felt. He still remembered to thank Mr. and Mrs. Argenta for the party, the gift, and the bread.

Beau walked out the front door into the snow. He carried his books in one hand, his new train in the other, and tucked the bread beneath his right arm. It was cold now, and the snow was falling in great, white, beautiful flakes. The ground was almost completely covered. Beau loved the snow. He always had a special feeling inside when it snowed. He could not exactly describe the feeling, but he felt warm and happy inside, and he was especially happy that his home was good and loving, and that his father would have built a big fire in the fireplace by now. He daydreamed about how warm it would be inside, and imagined that his mother would have a cup of hot cocoa for him. Just then, smack!! His happy thoughts were interrupted by a snowball that hit him in his left ear. He looked to see where it came from and he noticed Billy Grimes was behind a tree, laughing with his friends. Then, Billy started calling Beau names and making fun of him for getting the smallest loaf of bread. "Hey, Beau, I hope you don't get a stomachache from eating that huge loaf of bread. If you weren't such a weakling, maybe you could have gotten a real loaf, instead of a bite-size loaf." Then, Billy and his friends laughed and laughed; they were laughing so hard that they almost fell down in the snow. Beau bent over to make a few snowballs of his own to throw back at them. He threw three of them without landing one, but he was barraged by a whole fleet of white missiles. Smack!! Thwack!! They threw a few more snowballs at him, several hitting the intended targets, his head and chest. He was not injured. Not really. Only his pride was hurt, and being outnumbered, he just turned and walked away. He felt pretty stupid for getting the little loaf. He felt pretty stupid for getting ambushed. He thought to himself that Billy was probably right. He began to think how embarrassed he would be to present his little, crummy loaf of bread to his parents.

HE FINALLY MADE IT home, walked through the front door, left his shoes just inside the door, took off his coat, and told his parents he was home. He told them about the loaf of bread, and told them he should have pushed his way to the front of the line to get a bigger loaf. He felt like a failure.

His father encouraged him, "No, Beau. You did the right thing. I'm proud of you for being patient, for not shoving and pushing, and for allowing others to go first. Your loaf is just fine, and we'll enjoy it with our dinner tonight." Beau felt a little better. His father always made him feel better about things.

They sat down to eat in a few minutes. Beau's father prayed before they ate and thanked God for all the blessings he had given to them, for the food before them, and especially for the loaf of bread. In his heart, John Soleil was proud of Beau.

They passed the food around to each other, and Beau's father began to slice the loaf of bread. It *was* little, he thought, so he was careful to cut thin slices. About halfway through the slicing, he noticed that the knife was not cutting, and it made a scraping sound. *S-c-r-a-a-a-pe*. He thought there must have been a burned area of the bread, or maybe even a rock in it. He tried to cut it again, and felt and heard the same thing. *S-c-r-a-a-a-pe*. He turned the bread toward the lamp on the table to see the bread in better light, and he noticed something shiny in the middle of the loaf. He stopped cutting and reached his finger into the bread to discover the problem. It was not a problem. Not at all. The "problem" in the bread was both shiny and golden. There, buried in the bread, was a gold coin. He pulled it out, and looked closely at it. It was a twenty-dollar gold piece. He rolled it over in his hands, and felt the weight and the smooth surfaces. It reflected the light in the room in golden flashes. The coin was worth months of his labor. He thought the gold coin was there by accident. Possibly, somehow it had fallen out of someone's pocket while they made the bread. He didn't want to keep money that wasn't his, and he wanted Beau to know what honesty and truth required now.

John Soleil looked into Beau's eyes. "It looks like this little loaf of bread is slightly more valuable than you thought. What do you think we should do with this coin, Beau?" His father taught Beau by asking questions and by letting him try to solve problems.

Beau thought for a few seconds, and realized that if he wanted to keep the money, he could, and no one besides God and his family would know the difference. Finally, Beau spoke. "Daddy, this coin probably belongs to someone else. It's probably here by accident. I should go back to Mr. Argenta tomorrow and return it. It is probably his. I don't think we should keep it." He told his father that he would go back in the morning and give it back to Mr. Argenta.

John Soleil knew Beau was growing up.

BEAU GOT UP EARLY the next morning and looked outside. It had snowed all night and the whole town was covered as if it were wearing a great white overcoat. The snow made everything quiet and still. He remembered that today, he would see Mr. Argenta. He ate breakfast, got dressed, put the coin in his pocket, and went to the front door. He kissed his parents goodbye; they prayed with him, and then sent him out dressed in his warmest clothing.

Beau loved the snow. He loved the stillness and quietness it gave to the town. He loved the way it felt when he stepped forward. He loved the crunching sound it made as he walked. He loved the whiteness and brightness of it all. On the way to Mr. Argenta's house, he scooped up a handful of snow and ate it.

He arrived at Mr. Argenta's house and knocked on the door. Mrs. Argenta answered and Beau asked to see Mr. Argenta. Mrs. Argenta invited him inside. Soon, Mr. Argenta came to the entry hall and asked Beau to sit down with him in his office. Beau thanked him again for the party, for the train, and for the bread. He then explained the strange thing that had happened at dinner the previous night. He pulled the coin from his pocket and handed it to Mr. Argenta. Beau told him that somehow, accidentally, someone must have dropped the coin into the bread dough. "Mr. Argenta, I think this coin must be yours. I need to return it to you."

Mr. Argenta smiled, and then tears filled his eyes. He explained, "Beau, thank you for returning the coin. Every year at the Christmas party, we give out loaves of bread. In the smallest loaf, Mrs. Argenta places a twenty-dollar gold piece. We intend to give a special present to the child who is willing to allow others to go first. No one wants the smallest loaf, and since every other loaf is taken, only the child who is last gets the little loaf. And in that loaf, every year, is a gold coin. So you see, it is not an accident. I want one of you to have a special present each year. I want the special present to go to the one who is willing to let others go first. You are the first person who has ever come back to us to offer to give the coin back. The coin is yours, Beau. It is our gift to you. God bless you this Christmas and God bless you for your honesty."

Beau couldn't believe it. He stood up, accepted the coin from Mr. Argenta as he handed it back to him, and thanked him. Beau shook Mr. Argenta's hand and then hugged him. Mr. Argenta thought to himself, "Now there is a boy to watch. I want to see where he goes in life."

With great care, Beau placed the money in his pocket and walked home. He daydreamed about how happy his parents would be when he returned with the coin. He thanked God for this gift. Just before he got home, a snowball hit him in the head. Smack!! Oh, no. He saw Billy Grimes emerge from a stand of trees. Billy was grinning and yelling and making fun of Beau. Again.

But Beau could hardly hear him. He did not answer him with a word or a snowball.

Beau just smiled.

Beau loved the snow.

... the last shall be first, and the first last...
Matthew 20:16.

5

THE CONCERT

MR. ANDREW P. GRIMM, ESQUIRE was a very shrewd attorney.

He was one of five lawyers in Sure Hope. Four lawyers in town were honest men. Mr. Grimm was not numbered in that group.

Mr. Grimm was a man in his mid-forties with graying hair and beard. He was about 5'9" and he was clearly well fed. He liked being called Mr. Grimm, and often, because he insisted on introducing himself as "Andrew P. Grimm, Esquire," it was hard to know whether his last name was Grimm or Esquire. Some of the townsfolk actually called him Mr. Esquire. And worse, some of the mountain folk thought he gave his name as "Andrew P. Grimm, S. Squirrel" and took to calling him, in a deeply reverential tone, Mr. S. Squirrel, or, when in a hurry, Mr. Squirrel. As his facial appearance, with his whitish whiskers, unfeeling eyes, large ears, and elongated, narrow snout and mouth, was rather one that reminded people of a tree-dwelling rodent, the name "Mr. Squirrel" seemed appropriate. This alternative name eventually stuck.

No one really knew what the P. in his name stood for.

He was not a happy man; he rarely smiled and when he did, it was a sardonic smile. He was always seriously solemn, as if he harbored some deep hatred or some buried secret. No one knew much about him before he came to town twenty-five years earlier. Mystery seemed to surround him. He was wealthy and was well respected as a smart lawyer, but he was despised for his dishonesty, his harshness, his lack of integrity, and the utter inability of anyone to trust what he said. His fellow lawyers hated to go to trial against him. They hated to deal with him on even the most trivial matters because he was so unscrupulous.

Andrew P. Grimm, Esquire had made his fortune by taking any case people brought to him, regardless of merit. He would sue the innocent, he would sue the guilty, he would sue the rich, he would sue the poor, he would sue his friends, and he would have sued his own mother if he could have profited from it. It was fortunate for her that her death ten years earlier now kept her safely out of reach from this aggression. He would throw the poor off their farms and widows out of their homes if he could do it legally for his clients. He used the law as a blunt instrument of oppression rather than as a righteous weapon of justice.

In the end it was all for his benefit. He glossed over all of his misdeeds by repeating his favorite statement over and over again, heard by all in Sure Hope until they were sick of it: "My exalted duty is to be certain every man receives his just reward."

One never wanted to be on the receiving end of Mr. Grimm's tender mercies.

THE TOWN OF SURE HOPE feared and disliked Andrew P. Grimm, Esquire. But the inhabitants had more wisdom than Andrew Grimm. In fact, even the simplest citizen had more insight than he did. Everyone saw him for what he was: a proud, arrogant, selfish, pompous, conniving fool. He was an empty suit of clothing. No, it was worse than this. He was an emperor with no clothes.

People enjoyed making fun of him. He was the butt of many jokes, always told behind his back. Often, as he strutted along in town, children walked a few paces behind him, mimicking his strut and contorting their faces into a "grim" expression. With great glee, they called him Mr. Squirrel. Mischievous boys loved to play tricks on him. On one occasion, Beau Soleil and his friends found an old, empty purse. Hmm… what could they do with this? It must be useful for something. They hatched a plan.

Beau and the boys decided to trap Mr. Grimm in his own greed and dishonesty. They knew exactly when he left his office every day and they knew exactly which road home he took. They carefully timed and laid the trap. They strategically left the purse lying in the middle of the dusty road in a desolate stretch just a few minutes before Mr. Grimm would happen upon it. It appeared that the purse had fallen from someone's horse or wagon or buggy. Mr. Grimm could not fail to notice it. The boys counted on a predictable response from him. They hid in the woods just to the side of the road to observe the unfolding and exciting events.

The friends peered down the road with hungry anticipation. Sure enough, a few minutes later, Beau and his friends received their reward for patience. "Here comes Mr. Squirrel!" Beau whispered in barely contained excitement.

After a busy day of cheating others and deceiving himself, Andrew P. Grimm, Esquire came up the hill in his buggy at a slow pace as he meditated on his successes of the day. "What? What is this?" he thought. "A purse? A woman's purse in the middle of the country? Is God rewarding me for my upstanding life and my service to my fellow citizens?"

He slowed his horse to a stop. He looked around in every direction, making certain that no one saw him. And he quickly stepped down, retrieved the valuable object, hid it under a blanket, and then nonchalantly drove home as if nothing had happened.

The boys hiding in the woods watched all these events unfold and as they did, they looked into each other's laughing eyes; they could barely stifle a volcanic eruption. For they knew that Mr. Grimm would receive a great surprise when he arrived home. And they wished that they could be there to see his reaction. Why? It was because the boys carefully had perfumed the purse and just as carefully had stuffed the purse with a treasure Mr. Grimm would not want but one that was somehow fitting for a man of his great character. The treasure was something the boys had shoveled from the floor of a horse barn.

MATILDA GRIMM WAS Andrew Grimm's longsuffering wife of twenty-four years. She suffered long and she suffered much. Tillie Grimm had been the Sure Hope beauty of her generation, much desired by all the young men in town. Somehow, she had succumbed to the charms of Mr. Esquire and had given her heart and hand to him. Over the ensuing years, she had lost her beauty, her joy, and her life. He did not actually abuse her: he simply never loved her. He looked upon her merely as an ornament to the life of Andrew P. Grimm, Esquire. And Tillie Grimm wilted in the neglect, darkness, joylessness, and lifelessness of Mr. Grimm's home. She was now thin, gray, and sad, a middle-aged matron without any hope.

Melody was their only child. Her father spoiled her,

and in his twisted way, he loved her, almost as much as he loved himself. She had been given the best education in a Richmond finishing school, a seminary for wealthy young ladies of the Old Dominion. Now, at twenty-three years of age, she was married to Mr. William Manypenny, and she was returning to Sure Hope to live for good. Mr. Manypenny was a lawyer who would join Mr. Grimm's firm, working at first as a clerk and becoming a partner later if all went well.

Melody Grimm Manypenny was a singer. Well, at least she *thought* she was a singer. Her singing instructor in Richmond, Miss Tessa Tura, was a good musician, but had a great weakness for money and a great aversion to fits of pique. And Miss Melody had fits of pique with the best of them. She got angry whenever anyone disagreed with her, she got angry when anyone hurt her feelings, and she got angry when anyone told her anything she did not want to hear. During Melody's initial piano and voice lessons, Miss Tura tried to give her helpful correction. This constructive criticism always caused an outburst from Miss Melody during which she pounded the piano, bolted from the stool, threw sheet music onto the floor, ripped pictures off the wall, screamed, yelled, cried, and fell to the floor as if possessed. Miss Tura had considered that possibly it was time for a new teacher. However, she loved the money Mr. Grimm kept sending for the education of his precious, precocious daughter, and decided she would stick with Melody if the money kept flowing. It did. So she did. She accepted the bribe to keep teaching. And no matter what, she decided she would never cross Miss Melody again. It was a good deal all around.

Melody was an alto but had deluded herself into thinking she was a lyric soprano. Miss Tessa Tura never told her otherwise. Why risk a fit? They spent hours together with Miss Tura telling Melody exactly what she wanted to hear. Melody sang, usually flat; she was tone-deaf, just like her father. And she screeched when she was supposed to soar. It was not pleasant, but Miss Tura kept up her part of the bargain.

William Manypenny discovered Melody Grimm while visiting his sister at the seminary, and was immediately smitten by her beauty. He came from a wealthy Tidewater family, and he was not, to be charitable, especially... uh... intelligent. I mean, he was not really very bright. Well, that is being a little generous: he was actually exceedingly dull. He was not smart and he was not interesting, but he was nice and he was rich. And he had excellent eyesight. He could recognize a pretty girl when he saw one, and Melody was a pretty girl. And Melody could be persuaded by wealth.

They were made for each other.

WHEN THE MANYPENNYS arrived in Sure Hope, they were cautiously welcomed by the entire town. All the people of Sure Hope wanted to believe that Melody had changed in Richmond. She had—for the worse. The people of Sure Hope soon began to feel sorry for William Manypenny.

After the Manypennys had been in town for several months, her father arranged for and sponsored a concert at the church, the church building being the largest public area in Sure Hope. For many years, Mr. Grimm had done all he could to publicize his name. He had given money to sponsor special events, as long as they were called the Andrew P. Grimm, Esquire Lecture, Speech, Concert, etc. He had given funds for community buildings, as long as they featured a plaque: "Thanks to the Generosity of Mr. Andrew P. Grimm, Esquire." He was not generous, however. No. Not at all. He was self-serving and he was selfish, and he loved no one in the world more than Andrew P. Grimm, Esquire.

A concert thus offered another opportunity for self-aggrandizement. Who could resist that? Who could resist another chance to cover oneself in glory? Certainly not Andrew P. Grimm. This concert featured his daughter and he named it The Andrew P. Grimm, Esquire Concert Series. He was not sure when the next event in the series would occur, but he would figure that out later. The important thing was to get his name in front of the people. And... oh, yes… his daughter *was* a fine singer. A concert was just the thing to burnish his image and that of his family.

And so it happened that on October 27, 1877, the night of the concert, the people of the town began arriving early at Sure Hope Presbyterian Church, all of them dressed in their best clothes. There was much excitement and much chatter. Though no one liked Mr. Grimm or Mrs. Manypenny, they all hoped to hear some good music. The church was decorated in a festive manner and was illuminated by candlelight. On the piano and on tables at the front, there were vases of flowers shipped in from Richmond.

Twelve-year-old Beau Soleil arrived at the concert with his parents just before it began. Beau left his black Labrador retriever, Amos, outside the church to wait for him. His parents sat toward the back of the church, but Beau noticed that toward the front was his good friend, Wes Threlkeld. There were two other friends of theirs sitting with Wes, and Beau made his way to the front and squeezed in. Wes leaned toward Beau and in a low mock-serious tone, mumbled, "Beau, you are just in time. The Squirrel is about to appear." Beau giggled.

At precisely 7:30 p.m., Mr. Andrew P. Grimm, Esquire stood up and smiled an insincere, sardonic smile. He briefly welcomed one and all to the concert series that he was sponsoring. He waited for a round of applause as a sign of appreciation before he went on. He held up his hands and spoke again.

"Thank you, my friends. Again, it is with great pleasure that I welcome you to the inaugural event of the Andrew P. Grimm, Esquire Concert Series. I am humbled that I can give this gift of culture to you all. As you all know, and I say this humbly, not proudly, that humility is one of my chief virtues. At least that is what I am told. I humbly accept that appraisal. So, now, I humbly and proudly offer you this concert.

"It is my great privilege to present to you Mrs. Melody Grimm Manypenny, direct from Richmond where she has been studying voice for over three years with Miss Tessa Tura, a world-renowned expert in the vocal instrument. Mrs. Manypenny will perform pieces from Bach, Handel, and Mozart. For those of you who don't know, they are German and Austrian composers, and they are pretty good. And now, without further ado, here is my daughter, our singing angel, Mrs. Melody Grimm Manypenny!"

Beau elbowed Wes's side and whispered, "The Squirrel has spoken!" And then the church erupted in wild applause as Melody waltzed in. She was wearing a blue evening gown and her brown hair was held back by two ivory combs. Her pale skin shone, and the pearls around her neck seemed fitting. She was altogether a vision of beauty.

She smiled condescendingly and beatifically as she

thought to herself, "Now you yokels can hear some real music for the first time in your lives!" She cleared her throat and drank a little water. She cleared her throat again. She let her arms hang loosely at her sides.

On the piano, Mrs. Melisma began to play the introduction to a Mozart aria. The crowd waited in suspenseful anticipation for the first notes from Melody's golden voice. She appeared calm and her face was serene as she took a well-controlled deep breath, then effortlessly began to sing, eyes closed so as to savor the moment.

It was worse than awful.

Beau had never heard anyone sing so badly. Her notes were flat. And she screeched. And her screeching became flatter as she attempted to reach a high C. The audience was stunned. They were embarrassed for her. Their ears hurt. No one knew what to do. And Melody kept singing, eyes closed, oblivious to what was happening. She thought she was giving the performance of her lifetime for these simple townspeople.

Beau looked at Wes out of the corner of his eye. Both smiled. Beau began to giggle—just a little. Beau had excellent self-control.

But what was that noise? No, not the horrible singing. It was something else. "Oh, no!" Beau thought to himself. He began to hear dogs howling. It was Amos and his associates, just outside the church. Melody's singing was hurting the dogs' ears, and they were howling as if the moon were full. Melody had to compete with the dogs and it appeared that the dogs were winning.

Beau continued to giggle. He could not stop. He looked over at Wes and Wes was giggling and red-faced; he was holding his breath, attempting with all his might to stifle laughter. Wes punched Beau in the side with his elbow to try to get him to quit giggling. The singing was otherworldly—and I do not mean heavenly. There has never been singing in this world so utterly dreadful. The dogs accompanied Melody, singing back-up harmony. And Beau could no longer hold it in. His laughter burst out as if from an overinflated balloon. He began laughing so much it hurt. Both Wes and Beau were laughing now so hard that the pew was creaking and rocking. It was contagious. Their friends began to laugh. Soon, the entire audience was laughing and no one could stop. They had never heard anyone sing so terribly.

The singing, howling, and laughter made for utter chaos.

Melody finally stepped out of her music-induced trance, opened her eyes, and stopped singing. She surveyed the crowd. The sight of the entire audience laughing and the sound of the dogs howling were too much for her. She swept the vase of flowers from the piano to the floor, she trampled the flowers and shards of glass, and she ran out of the church, right into the arms of her husband William. She was devastated. They left quickly and went home, where she cried and whimpered all night. No one slept in the Manypenny household that night.

As the concert came to an abrupt halt, Andrew P. Grimm, Esquire rose to calm the crowd and make a few angry comments. His face was lavender as he chastised the audience for their lack of respect, their complete lack of appreciation of musical genius, their ingratitude, and their rudeness. He told them they were uncultivated, uncouth, uncivilized, and ill-mannered. They were backward, backwoodsy country bumpkins. He criticized their table manners, their indecorous dress, their poor grammar, their bathing habits, their bad breath—anything that came to mind. He even criticized them for chewing their food with their mouths open.

He finally finished his tirade, utterly spent, and slumped in a chair at the front. The crowd just sat there and realized they had just witnessed a first-class hissy fit.

But the excitement wasn't over yet. Oh, no. Not by a long shot.

As the crowd began to get up and leave, the sheriff burst through the rear doors of the church. He strode down the aisle to Mr. Grimm and said, "Andrew P. Grimm, Esquire, I have a warrant for your arrest. The State of Virginia accuses you of bank robbery in Richmond twenty-seven years ago."

The crowd was shocked. Mr. Grimm was shocked. His face was a deep purple now. He smiled (sardonically). He blustered something about being a good, upstanding, humble citizen. The sheriff handcuffed him and took him to jail to await his trial in Richmond.

And now the mystery cloaking Mr. Andrew Grimm, Esquire was revealed and he was laid bare.

It turned out that as an eighteen-year-old, Mr. Grimm was living in Richmond when he and a partner had robbed a major bank, carrying off $10,000 in silver dollars. The heist was so well planned that it had taken twenty-seven years to track him down. He had changed his name and had moved to Sure Hope after waiting long enough for the furor over the robbery to settle down. His given name had been Tertullus McGee.

He had never attended law school or read for the law. His diplomas and licenses were all fraudulent. How did they finally find him?

It so happened that William Manypenny had been interested in coins since childhood. Coins became his hobby and he became somewhat of an expert. His father-in-law paid him in silver dollars every two weeks for his clerking duties. Over time, William Manypenny was astute enough to notice the mint marking and date on the coins: the silver dollars all were marked with the exact same date and mint marking. All the coins were twenty-seven years old, marked with the year 1850. And they all were stamped with a P for Philadelphia. Was it a strange coincidence? It seemed a little unusual to him.

In addition, while doing some research for his father-in-law boss, he found a file tucked far back in the file cabinet with the name Tertullus McGee. And William Manypenny, not the shiniest coin in the purse, remembered his father having talked about a major bank robbery in Richmond that had occurred twenty-seven years before. He secretly went to Richmond to discuss his growing concerns with his father and the state attorney general, who just so happened to be an old family friend. Everything pointed to Andrew P. Grimm, Esquire as the criminal.

And Andrew P. Grimm, Esquire, also known as Mr. S. Squirrel, received his just reward from the State of Virginia. A state judge sentenced him to twenty years of hard labor in the state penitentiary and required him to make restitution to the bank for $10,000 plus interest.

No one in Sure Hope ever heard from him again or wanted to hear from him again, except for two people. His wife Tillie remained faithful to the end, visiting him often in prison until she died six years later. And daughter Melody, after enduring utter humiliation, became a young woman who was truly changed. Many in Sure Hope remarked that she became humble and appreciative of any kindness shown her. She also remained faithful to her father during his long prison years. Her marriage to William Manypenny flourished and they eventually had three children. Sadly, her singing never improved.

One mystery was never solved. No one ever knew what Tertullus McGee was thinking when he took on his new name, and he never revealed the secret even during his long years in prison. Did his middle initial P. mean anything at all? Was it chosen at random? Did he have some deep unconscious reason for choosing this initial? Did it stand for Proud? Pompous? Philadelphia? Prevaricator?

The mystery remains.

6

THE EAGLE

ALWAYS DEEPLY HIDDEN in the mountains of Virginia, Sure Hope was even more cloistered in the winter. From December through February, there was frequent snowfall and usually at least some snow on the ground. From the time he was a small child, Beau Soleil had reveled in the snow. In the warmth of his home, he sat at the window by the hour watching the big, wet flakes falling to the ground from the leaden gray skies, gradually accumulating in inches or even feet. Falling snow had a hypnotic effect on Beau. He felt at peace with the world. Noises disappeared, people stopped their scurrying about, and everywhere he looked he saw a brilliant white blanket covering the town and the surrounding mountains. Inside, his cup of hot cocoa in hand and encircled by his loving family, he had the feeling that all was well with the world.

There was something he loved even more than watching the snow and that was being outside *in* the snow.

Outside, he felt free, joyfully embracing the bitter wind as it peppered his red cheeks with icy flakes. He loved the challenge of being in the midst of cold weather.

He enjoyed making snowmen and snow angels, and he delighted in snowball fights. It was pure pleasure for Beau to scoop a glove-full of snow to his mouth and slake his thirst.

But Beau's favorite snow activity, far better to him than all the rest combined, was sledding. Sledding—he savored the thought and he exulted in the act. Many years before, his grandfather had handcrafted a sled of sturdy oak for his father, and now it had been handed down to Beau. He called it The Eagle because of the way it rapidly, silently, and effortlessly glided down the mountainside. He thrilled to the speed of The Eagle flying toward the valley below.

All was well in Beau's world in the silent Sure Hope winter.

BEAU'S GOOD FRIEND, Wes Threlkeld, lived with his family on a farm near the town. It was about three miles away. One cold January Sunday afternoon after church, Wes invited Beau to spend the day and night with him at the farm, and Beau readily accepted. Wes was fifteen years old by now, and Beau was thirteen. They drove to the farm in the family horse-drawn wagon and ate a bountiful lunch prepared by Mrs. Threlkeld. They gladly surrendered to fried chicken, mashed potatoes, string beans, and biscuits, followed by a generous slice of apple pie.

Then the friends bundled up and went sledding. Each of the boys had his wooden sled with wooden runners. They pulled the sleds up the mountain and came flying down to the road. It was an electrifying ride. The time went by quickly.

As dusk approached, they trudged to the Threlkeld farmhouse, utterly spent. They took off their boots and coats and barely made it to the floor in front of the fireplace before they collapsed there like tired old dogs. Their muscles ached and they felt exhausted—but exhilarated. They could barely get up off the floor when they were called to dinner. But they did manage to make it to the table. What teenage boy will refuse to eat?

After dinner, Mr. Threlkeld asked Wes if he would go down the road a short distance and make certain that the gate to the field was closed. The cattle were close to the barn, but he didn't want any of them to wander away during the night's expected new snowfall. It was dark by now, but the full moon illuminated the night sky and reflected off the snow so well it was almost as bright as day.

Wes and Beau decided to take their sleds. They got their winter gear back on and went outside, grabbed their sleds, and coasted to the road. Here, they got off and surveyed the road; it was empty and deadly still. With a running start, they flopped back onto their sleds and raced off down the hill. The gate was only a few hundred yards down the road, just around the corner, hidden by a stand of trees.

The quick trip to the gate was eerie. The moonlight was bright but everything shone in shadowy silver-sepia tones. The night was quiet and there was no wind. The only sound was the muffled swooshing of the sleds' runners.

They rounded the bend in the road and Beau raced ahead on The Eagle to the gate with Wes close behind. Beau turned to look at Wes to playfully taunt him for losing this race when suddenly Wes cried, "Beau, look out!!" Just in front of Beau was an old hay wagon parked on the side of the road. Beau had not noticed it, and he ran straight into the iron and wooden wheel. The sudden impact threw him off his sled and onto his back, and it knocked him out. He lay there lifeless, not moving at all.

The Eagle was in splinters. The snow around Beau was now a bright crimson, and his face was covered with blood. Wes saw it all happen and could do nothing to prevent it. He slid to Beau's limp body just seconds after the crash. His first thought was that Beau was dead. "Oh, no! Not that!" he thought. He felt a rush of deep horror unlike any he had ever experienced before.

Wes got off his sled and slipped on the snow as he walked to his unconscious friend's side. He was afraid to move Beau. He noticed Beau was breathing slowly. Beau had a long laceration on his forehead from his hairline to his nose. It was bleeding profusely. His nose was crooked and it was bleeding. His left jaw appeared to be misshapen. Wes pulled a clean handkerchief from his pocket and applied pressure to the bleeding wounds as he knelt beside Beau. He began to pray. "O God, please save Beau's life. Please, Lord, don't let him die. Jesus, help my friend!" He kept repeating the same prayer again and again.

After a few minutes, Beau began to move. It seemed like it had been an hour, but it was only three or four minutes. Beau moved, and then began to groan. Wes said aloud, "Thank you, Lord!"

Beau was hurting. He was confused. "Where am I? What happened?" he moaned. Wes tried to comfort him and help him to understand what had occurred. Wes knew he had to do something. Beau couldn't stay out in the cold for long, and Wes couldn't leave him here by himself to go for help.

Wes had to do something. He did the only thing he could do. He removed Beau's shattered sled and slid his own next to Beau. He gently slid Beau onto the sled, taking care not to move his neck, keeping him on his back. Fueled by God, by love for Beau, and by a surge of adrenaline, with heroic strength and will, he pulled Beau back up the hill on the sled to the Threlkeld farmhouse. God gives us adrenaline for times like this.

Wes and his badly wounded friend finally arrived at the farmhouse fifteen minutes later. Wes was barely able to stumble through the front door, and with gasping breath he cried, "Beau's hurt! Help!" Without a coat, his father rushed outside to where the boy was lying on the sled, still moaning, still incoherent. With extreme care and gentleness, Mr. Threlkeld and Wes each picked up an end of the sled with Beau still on it and carried Beau into the house. Enlisting the assistance of Mrs. Threlkeld and Matthew, their oldest son, they used a blanket to transfer him onto the kitchen table, pillowing his head with an old towel.

Beau looked even more ghastly in the light of the kerosene lamp.

Mr. Threlkeld immediately sent Matthew to fetch Doctor Andrew Davis from his home in nearby Tight Squeeze. Matthew saddled his horse and rode away into the night. Mrs. Threlkeld began to clean Beau's wounds, very carefully, with warm water and towels. The bleeding had stopped by now, but his face was swollen and his forehead was laid open to bone. Beau began to vomit, and Mrs. Threlkeld lovingly helped him turn his head as he did, cleaning out his mouth afterwards. Beau was still confused, but began to come around.

Matthew brought Dr. Davis to their home about an hour later. Matthew was then dispatched to the Soleil home. "Matthew," said his father, "do not alarm them. Tell them Beau has had an accident, but he is going to be alright. But tell them to come immediately."

Matthew left without stopping to warm himself by the fire.

DOC DAVIS WAS IN his late sixties. He had graying hair, keen brown eyes, and stooped shoulders that appeared to have borne many burdens. His hands were strong and gentle. His large frame made him seem intimidating until he smiled.

In Dr. Davis' many years of practice, he had seen everything. Nothing alarmed him and nothing surprised him. But when he walked into the Threlkelds' kitchen and saw the pale, bloodied, bruised, and swollen boy before him on the table, tears glistened in the old doctor's eyes. The boy was suffering excruciating pain and agony. Dr. Davis silently asked God for help, both for the boy and for himself.

It would be a long night.

After carefully washing his hands, the old doctor asked Beau if he knew where he was, and if he knew what had happened. Beau thought he was at home, and the last thing he remembered was sledding during the afternoon with Wes. Beau's pulse was rapid and weak, and Dr. Davis knew he had lost much blood. He saw no active bleeding and hoped all the hemorrhaging had stopped. He worried about whether he had bled into his brain, or whether he was now bleeding internally into his abdomen.

He was relieved that Beau's pupils were equal and reactive. With great care and gentleness, he examined Beau's scalp and skull. There was the obvious deep laceration of his forehead. He looked at his eardrums and there was no blood behind them. Beau's nose had stopped bleeding; despite the swelling, it looked fairly straight by now and would probably heal well. His left jaw was markedly swollen and deformed, and the doctor knew it was broken. His neck was not tender, not at all; it was not broken. His left mid-clavicle (collar bone) felt squishy and it hurt Beau as the doctor pressed on it; it was fractured, but Doc Davis knew it would heal. He listened carefully to Beau's heart and lungs with his stethoscope and they were normal. He was glad there was no injury there. His abdomen was not tender or distended. It appeared that all the trauma was from the neck up.

Dr. Davis washed his hands again and went to work. He told Beau that it would hurt, and then proceeded to clean his wounds. He tenderly and deftly cleaned the large forehead laceration. It was now apparent that the frontal bone (forehead) was broken. Dr. Davis began to suture the wound in layers as Beau drifted in and out of consciousness. He finished with twenty-seven stitches in the skin alone.

The next challenge was the jaw fracture. It would never heal unless it was immobilized. Dr. Davis ran some wire through Beau's teeth and wired his jaws together. Beau was beginning to awaken and become more alert. Beau asked him how he would eat. Doc Davis told him he would need to drink all his nutrition through a straw. Beau then had a frightening thought: what would happen if he had to vomit? He mumbled the question, and the good doctor never really answered.

Beau's parents arrived just as Dr. Davis was finishing his treatment. They were scarcely able to believe this was their son; he was bruised and battered almost beyond recognition. Hannah Soleil gasped when she saw her son and began to weep openly with quiet sobs, and John had tears streaming down his cheeks, both parents in anguish over their son's pain. But both quietly thanked God that Beau was alive. They rushed to their son's side as he lay there on the kitchen table and kissed him. They held his hands and he looked at them out of swollen eyes and smiled—slightly. They knew he would be alright.

Dr. Davis stayed another hour or so, continuing to observe his patient and to finish his treatment. He believed Beau would survive the skull fracture, concussion, and other injuries, and once he was satisfied that he was stable for the night, he gathered his instruments and prepared to leave. Before he left, he asked the family to pray with him.

The Soleils and the Threlkelds gathered around Beau and prayed silently as Doc Davis prayed aloud: "Father, thank you for Beau, and thank you for saving his life. Please heal him completely, and place your hand of blessing on him. Let him walk with you and serve you, and make him a blessing to you and others all his life. In Jesus' name, Amen."

Dr. Davis gave a few last instructions. "I'll be back tomorrow. Keep Beau quiet and comfortable. Let's move him to a bed here. He can't go home yet. He can have clear fluids to drink, and tomorrow, we'll start his liquid diet." With that, Dr. Davis went home, but not without an outpouring of thanks from both families.

Beau had a good night, and his parents attended him in the small bedroom the Threlkelds made available for them. He awoke the next morning with a bad headache, and he was still unable to remember what had happened to him. He relied on Wes's account of events the rest of his life. He drank some milk through a straw, and over the next few weeks, his mother had to call on all her ingenuity and creativity in feeding him what he needed through that straw. He would lose about ten pounds before he could eat normally again.

WHEN BEAU'S PASTOR HEARD about the accident the next day, he dropped all other obligations and went immediately to the Threlkelds' home. Reverend Thomas

Brooks McDonald was the minister of Sure Hope Presbyterian Church. He was a joyful man, about forty years of age, with piercing blue eyes and sandy-blond hair. He stood a lanky 6'5". His handshakes were legendary and bone-crushing.

Reverend McDonald had been born and reared in Lexington, Virginia. His family and community had experienced true revival there under the pastorate of William S. White. In addition, the revival had impacted many students at Virginia Military Institute and Washington College. Pastor McDonald later attended Hampden-Sydney College and Princeton Seminary, both hotbeds of revival in previous years. He was therefore steeped in the influence of the First Great Awakening and the Great Revival of Virginia. He was heir to the spiritual legacies of such men as Jonathan Edwards, Samuel Davies, William Graham, and Archibald Alexander. He had been touched and shaped by the gospel of grace of Jesus Christ; his heart was warm and his mind was sharp.

Reverend McDonald had been called to be pastor of Sure Hope Presbyterian Church when he was only twenty-five years old. He was the ideal pastor for this church which had been established in 1797 by descendants of Scottish, Scotch Irish, and French Huguenot settlers who were themselves sons and daughters of the Reformers. Upon arrival to the lush valley, the settlers had named the town Sure Hope. The name of the town was a reference to and a reminder of God's utter trustworthiness, as found in Hebrews 6:18-19:

> … *That by two immutable things, in which it was impossible for God to lie,*
>
> *we might have a strong consolation,*
>
> *who have fled for refuge to lay hold upon the hope set before us:*
>
> *Which hope we have as an anchor of the soul, both sure and stedfast…*

Revival had come to the church and the community in the 1850s, as it had to Lexington, and had spread throughout the Shenandoah Valley. The revival had been preceded by the fervent prayers of many believers. The revival had been real, not man-made or contrived. It had occurred through the usual gifts God gives the church: preaching of the Word of God, corporate worship, and the sacraments. However, the Holy Spirit had worked through these usual means with extraordinary power and swiftness. Only the Holy Spirit can bring revival.

As a result of the widespread revival, many hearts in Sure Hope and in western Virginia had been changed, and the results were obvious as people began to treat each other as Christ would. Love for Jesus and love for others reigned.

Individuals, families, churches, towns, and communities were transformed by the gospel of Jesus Christ. The results remained. Pastor McDonald was a good shepherd to his church. He led them, guarded them, and fed them well as he preached the Bible with conviction and passion. He loved his people and his people loved him.

AS REVEREND MCDONALD walked into Beau's room, he immediately recognized that Beau's suffering was great, and Beau's pain penetrated the pastor's own heart. He had known Beau since he was a baby. He had baptized him. He had taught him the Westminster Shorter Catechism (which begins: *What is the chief end of man? Man's chief end is to glorify God, and to enjoy him forever*).

Beau heard him come in. He opened his eyes, smiled weakly, and mumbled a greeting. "Hello, Mr. McDonald. What brings you here?" The pastor was glad to hear Beau felt like joking. He reached for Beau's hand and held it in his. He asked Beau how he was feeling, and he told him about an accident he himself had had as a young boy on the farm. He read a few verses to him from Psalm 103:

> *Bless the Lord, O my soul: and all that is within me, bless his holy name.*
>
> *Bless the Lord, O my soul, and forget not all his benefits:*

Who forgiveth all thine iniquities; who healeth all thy diseases;

Who redeemeth thy life from destruction;

Who crowneth thee with lovingkindness and tender mercies;

Who satisfieth thy mouth with good things; so that thy youth is renewed like the eagle's ...

... The Lord is merciful and gracious, slow to anger, and plenteous in mercy.

Reverend McDonald prayed with him before he left. He promised to come back to see Beau often, and he kept his promise. He also prayed for Beau each Sunday from the pulpit until he was well.

DR. DAVIS CAME BY to see Beau every day for a week, checking his wounds, re-bandaging him, and making sure his patient was improving. After a few days, he gave permission for Beau to go home, so they loaded him into the wagon and drove him to town. The sun was shining, but it was a frigid winter day and snow lay on the ground in three-foot drifts.

Dr. Davis was a humble physician who knew his job was to do all in his power to help Beau heal. He also knew his limitations: he knew he never actually healed anyone.

He realized that Jesus was the great healer and that a doctor's part was to treat a patient with attentive skill, gentle compassion, and kind tenderness. And he could pray for his patients. He did his job well. He talked with Beau about everything you can think of. He playfully teased him. He answered Beau's questions. He allayed his fears.

ONCE HOME, BEAU NEEDED full-time care for the next week or so. Hannah and John Soleil gladly gave it. John moved him and helped make him comfortable. Hannah continued to be creative in Beau's nutrition, being sure that he received what he needed to heal. She blended his food by hand and then used a straw to deliver it through his wired jaws. She changed his bandages, she gave him bed baths, and she sat with him for hours. She told him stories of her family, of the morning they discovered him, of The War Between the States. She read him the Bible. He enjoyed hearing her read about the kings of Israel. Even more, he loved to hear his mother read the story of Jesus in the Gospels. The Gospel of Mark became his favorite book in the Bible. He liked the fast pace, and he loved the reality of Jesus as he stepped forth from the pages of Scripture.

WHEN GRACE MCLEOD HEARD the bad news about Beau's accident, she was distraught and could not control her tears. She was twelve years old then, and she had not changed except that she was now growing into comely womanhood. Her hair was still brown, now with a hint of red, and her gaze was still penetrating. Her emotions still burned with fire. Her intense love still controlled her. And she still thought Beau Soleil was the best boy in the world.

So when Grace heard about Beau's injuries, her heart broke for him. She could not bear the thought of his suffering and could not even entertain the idea that he might have died on that moonlit night. She begged her parents to take her to see Beau at the Threlkelds' home.

Her father sat down with Grace, his arm around her, and explained, "Gracie, I know how much you care for Beau. I've talked with his father. Beau was badly injured in the sledding accident, but he will recover with God's help. What he needs now is your prayers, and he needs rest. He is in a lot of pain and he can't have visitors yet. I know he would like to see you. You always bring him cheer. But let's wait until he's feeling a little better and returns home. You can see him then, I promise. Why not just write him a note now telling him you're worried about him and you're praying for him?"

Grace was disappointed but she knew her father was right. She went to the kitchen table, wrote a short note in blue ink with neat script, folded it, and asked her father to give it to Beau's parents to deliver to Beau.

Beau's mother read him the note from Grace the next day.

Dear Beau,

I'm sorry you got hurt.
I am praying for you.
I can't wait to see you.
Get well soon.
Your friend,

Grace

He listened carefully and he smiled just a little; his wired jaws made it difficult to smile. But his heart was smiling broadly with joy at hearing from Grace. He could feel her gentle caring in the words. Grace. Sweet Grace.

THE VERY DAY BEAU arrived back home, Grace came to his house and visited him. She was impatient to see how he was doing. As she walked into his room with Beau's mother, even though she had been warned that he looked awful, she could hardly bear the sight of his bruised, swollen face. Tears filled her eyes as she made her way to his bedside and took his hand. Beau had drifted off to sleep but he awakened to see Grace's bright face looking on in deep concern. He attempted to smile as he looked into her expressive eyes.

"Beau, are you hurting much?" she asked.

"A little. Don't worry, Grace. I'll be fine," he mumbled.

For the next fifteen minutes, Grace stayed with him,

holding his hand, praying for him, as he went back to sleep in peace. As she left, unbeknownst to him, she gave him a kiss on his cheek.

Tender Grace would return almost every day until Beau fully recovered. As she sat with him, she talked when he felt like listening and sat quietly when he needed rest. She simply kept him company when he napped. She helped Beau's mother attend to his needs.

One afternoon, soon after Beau began to doze, Grace noticed that he seemed agitated. He began to thrash in the bed, to moan and then cry, then scream as if he were terrified. It frightened Grace and she called for Hannah. "Mrs. Soleil, please come quickly! Something's wrong with Beau!"

Hannah Soleil rushed into the room and recognized that Beau's dream had returned. She gently prodded him and he awakened, drenched in sweat. He seemed confused and scared. He realized that Grace was sitting beside him, and he was embarrassed.

"Grace," he said as he turned to her, "I'm sorry." Beau spoke as clearly as he was able through his wired teeth. "I know this frightened you. I had a bad dream. The worst of it is that this same dream keeps coming back, and it tortures me. Every time, I see a young woman roaming in a dark, snowy woods. She is so sad and she is carrying a burden. I do not know if it means anything at all, but it terrifies me and confuses me and makes me sad."

Grace placed her hand on his and gently responded, "Beau, I'm sorry this dream keeps coming back. But it is only a dream. And now you are safe in your bed. You will be fine." Gentle Grace understood. She always seemed to know what to say and she rarely got flustered or panicked. Beau relaxed and went back to sleep.

As Beau improved over the next few weeks, Grace brought him a present. It was John Bunyan's classic, *The Pilgrim's Progress*. Grace read it to Beau by the hour and they talked about it during breaks from the reading. It became their favorite book as they together followed Christian's difficult path to The Celestial City.

And Beau and Grace's friendship deepened.

SOON AFTER BEAU ARRIVED back home, Dr. Davis brought an imposing friend with him to see Beau, a surprise visitor. The visitor was tall, about 6'3", and somewhat frail.

"Beau," said Dr. Davis, "I want you to meet someone. This is Dr. Barnabas Trust. He is home from Richmond for a few days visiting his family in Winchester. I've known his father, Dr. Silas Trust, for a long time; we were medical school classmates. I met Barnabas when he was a mere baby. He went to medical school in Philadelphia and stayed there for an extra year for additional training. Now Dr. Barnabas Trust is a world-renowned surgeon. He has just begun a new medical school in Richmond."

Dr. Trust was moved when he saw Beau's healing but still-battered face. He smiled and put out his hand to shake Beau's as he approached his bed. "How're you feeling, Beau? Sounds like you had a pretty close scrape."

Beau took Dr. Trust's hand and smiled. "I'm feeling better, Dr. Trust. I know I look bad, but I'm feeling better."

"Beau, you will heal. With God's help and Dr. Davis' attention, you will get better. It helps that you are so young. Children and young people always heal quickly. The next time I see you, you will be completely normal."

"Thank you, Dr. Trust. This is good news. Thank you for stopping by to see me," Beau replied.

"Beau, it is my pleasure to see you. I was wondering: Have you ever considered that you might be called to be a physician and surgeon? I've just begun a new medical school. From everything Dr. Davis tells me, you would make a fine doctor. Maybe you'll eventually wind up in Richmond with me as one of your professors."

"I have thought about medicine. I know it requires a long, expensive education." Beau still struggled to clearly enunciate his words through wired teeth and jaws. He was only partially successful, but he got his point across.

Dr. Trust thought for a few seconds. "Beau, if you think God is calling you to become a physician, then pursue it. God will provide for you if he has called you. Think and pray about it. And let me know if you ever want to attend medical school in Richmond."

Beau thanked Dr. Trust and took his advice to heart. No one said a word for a minute or so until Dr. Davis spoke up, "Beau, let's take a look at my favorite patient."

Dr. Davis did a quick exam. Beau was improving rapidly. Then both physicians left. Dr. Trust's last words to Beau were, "God bless you, Beau. Get well. Think about becoming a doctor. The new medical school is called The University School of Medicine. I hope to see you there someday."

ABOUT A WEEK AFTER Beau's homecoming, Doc Davis began coming by every few days, and then, as Beau healed, the visits came to an end. Over time, Beau's stitches had been removed, his jaws had been unwired, his nose had healed straight (almost), and his clavicle had developed a large bony swelling in the middle that would resolve over time. Even his black eyes were gone. Beau was grateful to be able to eat again. He had lost about ten pounds and he was weak, but now, with unwired jaws, he ate like three teenage blacksmiths, and his strength returned.

BEAU RETURNED TO school after a month, and all his friends welcomed him back with a party. Life became normal again, though he would not fully heal for months.

During the long weeks of recovery, Beau had many hours to think and pray. Beau made an important decision:

he decided his future lay in medicine. He wanted to help others the way Dr. Davis had helped him. And from that time, Beau aimed his whole life toward becoming a physician, caring for people in the name of Jesus Christ.

AS FOR SLEDDING—his father made him a new sled that summer. It was even better than The Eagle. It had hickory runners covered in smooth wrought iron. The Eagle II would be a fast sled.

And it snowed in the mountains every winter.

7

THE PROPOSAL

CHRISTMAS WAS BEAU SOLEIL'S favorite day of the year. Christmas in 1880 was no exception—except that Beau turned sixteen that day and the celebrations were even better than usual.

Beau had become a man. He had worked with his father in the blacksmith shop since he was little. Now, trained by his father, Beau was almost as expert in the smithy as John Soleil. Beau had grown in the past two years. He now stood a full 6'3" and weighed 205 pounds. His enormous appetite in combination with the constant lifting and hammering in the shop had added pounds of muscle to his chest, arms, forearms, and hands. Beau's upper body strength was as real as it was apparent.

CHRISTMAS EVE THE SOLEILS had gone to church to celebrate the birth of Jesus Christ. A fresh blanket of snow had fallen that afternoon and the world was quiet and still. Wreaths suffused the air in the church with their earthy pine scent. Red and white candles burned dimly. Mrs. Melisma played Christmas carols on the piano and families entered the church together, greeting each other as they filled the pews. Beau looked around and nodded at Wes Threlkeld. As Beau took his place, he continued looking around for the person he really wanted to see. She finally walked in with her family. Grace McLeod had arrived. Beau could not stop gazing at her. Her brown hair was pulled back in a white ribbon, her brown eyes sparkled in the candlelight, and she wore a red velvet dress with a white ribbon tied in a bow around her waist. She was the picture of simple, elegant beauty. Beau kept gazing at her until Grace glanced at him and smiled. He answered with an embarrassed smile, acting as if he were simply surveying the room and had accidentally encountered her eyes.

The worshipers prayed, gave thanks, sang Christmas carols, and heard a sermon by Pastor McDonald. They ended the service by singing Beau's favorite carol, "Joy to the World." It was good to celebrate the birth of Jesus Christ, Savior and Redeemer of the World.

Before they left the church that night, Beau made a point to speak with Grace. He wished her Merry Christmas and as she returned the greeting, her searching eyes peered into his eyes and completely disarmed him. She always seemed to know exactly what he was thinking. She smiled at him and they both went to their homes.

BEAU AWAKENED EARLY CHRISTMAS morning to the welcome aroma of hot coffee. His mother was already up, making breakfast pastries. As Beau stumbled into the kitchen, he was offered some black coffee (he always drank it black—why ruin coffee by putting contaminants in it?) and a pastry. His mother wished him Merry Christmas and happy birthday and greeted him with a kiss. He knew it would be a good day.

The Soleils finished breakfast. Beau and John did some necessary chores as Hannah stayed inside cooking the Christmas feast. Beau and his father returned inside at about noon, kicking snow off their boots and brushing snow off their coats. They were cold and the fire was hot. They both pulled chairs to the hearth to warm themselves.

"Hannah, dinner smells good. We can't wait, can we, Beau? I could eat an elephant." John Soleil usually said he could eat a horse unless he was really hungry or the food smelled better than usual, and then he chose a bigger animal. The elephant seemed to fit this time. Sometimes, he wanted to eat cows, hippopotamuses, or rhinoceroses.

"John and Beau, we'll eat in about fifteen minutes. Get yourselves warm and then come to the table." Hannah had prepared a feast. There was ham, turkey, mashed potatoes, biscuits, green beans, and fruit (canned last summer). And of course, Hannah had made her famous cherry pie.

They all soon moved to the table and as they sat down, they bowed their heads as John prayed. "Lord, we thank you for this day. Thank you for your Son, Jesus Christ. Thank you for our son, Beau. And thank you for the feast that Hannah has made for us. In Jesus' name, Amen."

They all said "Amen" and then both Hannah and John wished Beau a happy sixteenth birthday.

They ate the elephant for the next hour and then sat by the fire to talk while sipping cups of hot chocolate.

They heard a knock at the door. Beau went to answer the knock and opened it to see Mr. and Mrs. Argenta standing in the snow. "Come in, Argentas! Merry Christmas!!" Beau greeted them heartily. He liked this couple. He loved this couple.

"Merry Christmas, Beau! And happy birthday!" Mr. and Mrs. Argenta answered in unison.

They entered the Soleil home and exchanged greetings. Mrs. Argenta gave the family some of her Christmas cookies, and Hannah gave them some pumpkin bread.

They visited for about twenty minutes. Mr. Argenta was usually fairly quiet unless he had something to say. He leaned forward in his chair. He wanted to talk about something serious. Mr. Argenta was not one for small talk.

"John, Hannah, Beau, we've been talking about

something and I want to present it to you. We think you may find it interesting."

"This sounds intriguing," Beau said after a few seconds of silence. He reached his left hand into his pocket and began to fiddle with his brass button. He had begun to always carry it with him by this time.

"Beau, what do you intend to do when you finish school this spring?" The question posed by Mr. Argenta was a regular topic of conversation in the Soleil household.

"Mr. Argenta, I want to go to college—eventually. After that, I want to go to medical school—eventually. That's been my dream ever since my sledding accident. My only problem is money. My grades are excellent. I have studied hard and I've done well. But I don't have the money for more schooling yet. I plan to work with my father for a few years and save everything I can. Then, I plan to go to college. Somewhere. Sometime." Beau's voice trailed off as he realized the difficult road ahead.

"Beau, I may have a solution for you. Mrs. Argenta and I think you will become a fine physician. You have the intellect, you have the temperament, you have the character, and you have the love for people.

"What would you say if I offered you a deal? I have a proposal for you."

Beau was listening carefully. Mr. Argenta held out hope for Beau, and he could barely restrain his excitement.

"Please go on, Mr. Argenta." Beau appeared calm but he was anything but calm. His brass button was getting hot from being handled; friction can produce a lot of heat.

"Here's what I am thinking, Beau. Sure Hope needs a doctor. Dr. Davis just turned seventy and may not be working much longer; he won't work forever. He is slowing down. You want to be a doctor but have no money. I'm getting old and want to do something for Sure Hope that will last. I'd also like to do something for you and your family. I've watched you grow up, and I'm convinced you have a great future ahead of you.

"So here is my proposal. It is really pretty simple. Suppose I pay your way to college and medical school with the understanding that you return home once you finish and take care of the folks of Sure Hope? I see this as a triple win."

Beau was stunned. He could not believe that Mr. Argenta would do something like this. He had a reputation for generosity, but this offer, as Beau understood it, was far beyond generosity.

"Please let me be sure I understand, Mr. Argenta. Are you saying that you would pay all my expenses if I come back here to practice?"

"Yes, Beau, that is exactly what I am saying. The only risk you would run is this: if you decide not to come back, you would agree to pay the money back to me as a loan.

But if all works as planned, this will benefit everyone. We get a doctor, you get your education quickly, and I leave something important for our town." Mr. Argenta was careful to present the deal as good for him, good for the town, and good for Beau. He did not want to insult Beau or make him think he was unable to eventually get to his goals by himself.

"Mr. Argenta," Beau responded, "I think we may have a deal. May I have a few days to think and pray about this, and to discuss it with my parents? Your offer is most kind and generous. Thank you for being willing to do this for me. I am grateful."

Mr. Argenta answered, "Beau, you can have all the time you need to answer me. I know this is sudden. I hope it works out. Please let me know." And turning to Hannah, he said, "Now Hannah, I have been admiring the cherry pie on the table since we arrived. Do you think I might have a small slice?" As we have seen, Mr. Argenta only spoke when he had something important to say, and cherry pie is an important topic to discuss.

Hannah arose from her chair, cut him a slice, and placed whipped cream on top. He thanked her for it as she handed it to him. The rest of the conversation was light and breezy. The Argentas left soon afterwards.

THREE DAYS LATER, Beau paid a visit to Mr. Argenta's home. He talked with Mr. Argenta in his office where he again expressed his gratitude for the offer. He told Mr. Argenta that he accepted and looked forward to the time when he returned to practice medicine in Sure Hope. They shook hands on it, and then Mr. Argenta gave Beau a big hug. There was no written contract: they were men of honor and their word was their bond.

"Beau, before you leave, I have one more thing for you to think about." Mr. Argenta had been busy in the days since Christmas. "Beau, a good friend of mine is president of Huguenot College, near Richmond. We've discussed your situation. He tells me you can start there in September if you would like to."

Beau was filled with gratitude to have someone like Mr. Argenta as his champion. "Thank you, Mr. Argenta. Thank you. I won't disappoint you."

"I know you won't, Beau. I have great confidence in you."

They shook hands once more and Beau stepped outside into the cold and snow. He took a deep breath and looked upward. "Thank you, God. Thank you!"

BEFORE HE WENT HOME, there was one person Beau wanted to see. He had to see Grace and tell her his good news. He walked to the McLeod home and knocked on the front door. Grace answered and opened the door and smiled. Her eyes looked into Beau's and she knew he had something on his mind.

"Good morning, Beau," she said. "Come on in. It's cold outside."

"Good morning, Grace. No, I think I'd rather stay outside. Actually, it's beautiful outside. Can you please come for a walk with me? I have something important to tell you."

Grace went back inside and asked her parents if she could go. She came out in a few minutes in her coat and scarf and waited for Beau to speak as they walked away from the house.

"Grace, I have wonderful news. I'm going to college and medical school."

"I know you want to become a doctor, Beau. Is there something new?"

Then Beau explained the whole thing to Grace, from Sure Hope to Huguenot College to medical school to Sure Hope again.

The usually calm and reserved Beau was as excited as Grace had ever seen him. She shared his joy and told him, "Beau, I am so happy for you!" And with a sudden impulse, she hugged Beau and kissed him on the cheek.

Beau hugged her for a second and looked into her eyes. Then he kissed her cold, rosy cheek. He thought to himself, "Someday, I'm going to marry that girl."

Beau walked Grace back home and then ran home, as fast as you can run through snow, to tell his parents of the morning's new development.

And as he ran, he again looked heavenward and said aloud to God, "Thank you, Lord!"

And then he talked to himself, again, out loud: "Beau, someday, you are going to marry that girl."

8

HUGUENOT COLLEGE

BEAU SOLEIL BEGAN HIS long path toward becoming a physician in September 1881. After a delightful summer in Sure Hope, working hammer and tongs with his father as a blacksmith, spending time with Dr. Davis as he tended patients, and enjoying his fleeting time with Grace, Beau traveled to Richmond with his father and mother. Beau's work in the blacksmith shop, combined with prodigious helpings of Hannah's cooking, had added even more muscle and strength to his large frame. He stood 6'4" and weighed 210 pounds. He was a stout sixteen-year-old man.

Travel to Richmond was fairly easy. A stagecoach to Winchester and a train to Richmond transported them in a few hours. Once in the city, they went directly to Huguenot College, on the outskirts of Richmond, and Beau looked in wonder at the stately buildings, the spacious lecture halls, and the immaculate grounds. He had never seen anything like this before.

A room on campus had been reserved for Beau. John, Hannah, and Beau carried his belongings to his room and organized things. Beau was meticulous and fastidious; he loved order and worked best in an orderly atmosphere. It was worth time and effort to set things up well from the start. Clothes were arranged neatly in the wardrobe. Pens, paper, and books were placed just so on his desk. His bed was properly made. Books were arranged by author on the bookshelf.

Beau's roommate was Mark Talbot, a young man from Norfolk, who arrived a few hours later. Both Beau and Mark wanted to become physicians. They would become good friends and study mates over the next four years.

After touring the campus, and after discovering the location of the all-important dining hall, Beau said goodbye to John and Hannah. Beau embraced and kissed his parents and they him. John prayed for God's blessing on his beloved son. Before he turned to leave, John gave Beau some parting words.

"Beau, your mother and I are proud of you and we love you. You will do well here. Remember always to follow the Lord. Rely on him for wisdom. Work hard. Do your best. Try to write often. Remember: you belong to God."

"Daddy and Mama," Beau responded, "I love you both, too. I'll miss you. Thank you for allowing me to come to college."

Hannah by this time was crying. She had decided beforehand that she would not cry, at least not until she had left Beau. But she couldn't help it. She turned to hide her tears from Beau but couldn't conceal them. Beau and John both mightily controlled their emotions as everyone hugged once more. But as they turned from each other, there were tears in everyone's eyes.

Then John and Hannah were gone. Beau was on his own for the first time in his life. And that night as he tried to sleep, his heart hurt him. He had never felt this sensation before. Sleep finally overtook him after midnight.

THE NEXT DAY ALL incoming freshmen gathered to hear from Dr. Archibald Robertson, the president of the college. Dr. Robertson was an old friend of Mr. Argenta. He gave the usual warm welcome to the new students and gave them instructions about meeting with academic advisors later that morning. Just afterwards, Beau went to the front of the room to meet Dr. Robertson.

He introduced himself. "Dr. Robertson, my name is Beau Soleil. I'm from Sure Hope. Mr. James Argenta is a friend of mine. He told me you and he were good friends and that I should introduce myself to you."

Dr. Robertson responded by grasping Beau's outstretched hand and with a warm smile replied, "Well, Beau, I have been looking forward to meeting you. James

Argenta is a dear friend and he has told me all about you. He speaks very highly of you. I'm glad to finally meet you and I'm glad you are here with us. If I can ever assist you, please call on me."

"Thank you, Dr. Robertson. Thank you for your welcome and for your kind offer. I hope to do well here and will give it my best effort," Beau answered.

"I'm sure you will, Beau. Again, welcome." Dr. Robertson turned to greet another student, and Beau walked to his advisor's room.

CLASSES BEGAN TWO DAYS later, and from the beginning Beau carried a heavy load. He soon realized that many other students were far ahead of him. In his first year, he studied Greek, chemistry, history, Bible, and calculus. He struggled to keep up.

He enjoyed his new friend and roommate. Mark Talbot was a small-framed young man. He was a member of one of the First Families of Virginia. He was intelligent, cultivated, and sensitive. He was well-connected. Yet Mark was not proud. He enjoyed getting to know Beau, and Beau learned much from Mark.

Soon after their arrival on campus, a friend of Mark's came by their room to visit Mark. He was an upperclassman named Pete Jones. His full name was Gustave Wilfred Wingfield Danegeld Pierre Jones VI. Someone many years before had thought this name was a good idea for his remote ancestor, Gustave Wilfred Wingfield Danegeld Pierre Jones I. This all-inclusive name would combine every important family name, from all the ages, into one. The length of the name had caused much difficulty for its bearers over the years. The ever-increasing suffix caused people to wonder if the Jones men were of some royal lineage. Not one of the Jones men ever denied the possibility. The Jones men blessed with this name became good explainers and excellent fighters. Pete Jones despised his name and never used it unless he had to. Before he came to Huguenot, his family had called him Pierre. But when he began college, he threw Pierre overboard and told everyone to call him Pete. Because he was oversensitive and even defensive about his own pretentious name, he made it his hobby to persecute others with unusual names. A good offense is the best defense.

Pete Jones was from Williamsburg. He and Mark had been friends since childhood, back when Pete was known as Pierre. Pete's father was a well-known Virginia politician. Young Pete Jones thought he deserved a lot of respect.

Pete entered the room and asked Mark how he liked college. Before Mark had time to answer, Pete noticed Beau sitting at his desk, studying.

"Mark, who's your friend?"

"Pierre…" Mark started to introduce Beau before he was interrupted by Pete.

"Mark, call me Pete. I'm Pete now. Remember? Don't call me Pierre."

"Sorry, Pete. I forgot you were not Pierre anymore. Pete, this is Beau Soleil. He's from Sure Hope. He plans to become a doctor." Mark was humble and soft-spoken as always.

Beau turned around in his chair to meet Pete.

Pete spoke with arrogance and insolence as he spoke to Beau. "What?? *What's* your name, boy? Boo So-Low? Or Boo Solell? Huh? Isn't that a fancy name for a country boy?"

"My name is pronounced Bo Sol-A. It's French." Beau replied coolly, patiently, and good-naturedly. Beau reached into his pocket and began fingering his button. He turned it over several times as he waited for the conversation to continue.

"Yes, I know your name is French. But I think I'll call you Boo. Yes, Boo So-Low. You *are* a country boy, aren't you?"

"Yes, I'm from a small town on the Shenandoah River." Beau stayed calm. He kept playing with the button.

"Well, Boo. I hope you make it here. I hope you're not as stupid as you look and talk."

Here Mark intervened. "Pete, don't insult my friend. Beau doesn't deserve it and you have no right."

To which Pete replied, "I have a right to say anything I please and to insult anyone I want. I'm a Jones. Do you know who my daddy is?"

Beau had controlled himself and tried to laugh along. He realized a fool had just entered his room. Yet even a patient, self-controlled young man like Beau had his limits.

Pete was too full of himself and too blinded by pride to stop taunting Beau. Besides, Pete Jones was not the brightest of collegians. He turned to go and as he did, he leveled one more insult. "Goodbye, Mark. Take care of this country boy roommate of yours. Boo. Boo So-Low. How low can you go, Boo? Boo So-Low. What a name!!" Pete laughed at his own humor and wit. He was having fun.

Leaving the room, Pete launched one last verbal missile at Beau. "Boo…no…I don't think you'll make it here." He laughed again. He walked out.

Pete was startled to hear a sudden thunderclap behind him. He turned around and saw that Beau had sent his fist crashing down on his desk like a blacksmith's hammer on his anvil. Pete stood looking and Beau stood up. Beau walked towards him. Mark saw what might happen and he grabbed Beau by his shoulders and hung on as he said, "No, Beau! No!!" Mark did not like violence—or blood. Beau kept walking, dragging Mark with him.

Beau walked to Pete, stood over him, and looked down on him for a few uncomfortable moments. He spoke softly and slowly, with no need to raise his voice, "Who… do you… think… you're talking to?" With a steady, angry gaze and without a smile, Beau looked down into Pete's fearful eyes. Beau's fists were clenched.

Even someone as oblivious as Pete knew he had overstepped his bounds. He felt very small in Beau's shadow. Even Pete had the sense to know that he was in the presence of his physical—and moral— superior.

Beau never touched Pete—he didn't need to. But he made his point. Pete mumbled an apology and told Beau he was sorry for insulting him. He never did again, at least to his face. He never called him Boo again. He did, however, give him a new nickname. From then on, when Pete saw Beau, he called him "Hammer." And the nickname Hammer stuck. For the next four years, Huguenot students used the names Beau and Hammer interchangeably for the young man from Sure Hope.

FOUR WEEKS INTO THE school term, Beau realized that the heart-sick feeling he had experienced the first night at college had a name: homesickness. The feeling was always present, though it varied in intensity. He missed his family and his friends. He missed Sure Hope. Most of all, he missed Grace.

He wrote to his parents and Grace at least once a week. He told them everything was going well. He did not want them to worry. But it was not going well. Not at all. He was failing three courses. He was staying up late to study, so late that he could not stay awake in class the next day. Then he had to go to the library, and later to his room, to teach himself everything he should have learned from professors in class that day. There were new assignments in addition. It was a bad cycle. He was working as hard as he could and it was not enough.

Beau began to think that he should have stayed home in Sure Hope. Maybe he did not belong in college. He doubted himself and his abilities. He feared failure. He feared disappointing all the people who had helped him and who had believed in him. He thought of his father and mother, of Mr. Argenta, and most of all, he thought of Grace. What would they all think if he failed out of college and came home? How could he face them again? What if he never achieved his goal of becoming a physician? Doubt, fear, anxiety, and shame began to erode any inner peace and joy.

BEAU DECIDED TO PAY a visit to President Archibald Robertson. Dr. Robertson had invited him to ask for his help if he ever needed it. Beau accepted his invitation. He needed help. He was drowning.

At the appointed day and time, soon after lunch, Beau went to Dr. Robertson's office and waited on a bench in the hall until his appointment. It was a warm autumn day. A large grandfather clock in the hallway told him it was 1:05 p.m. Beau listened to the hypnotic swinging of the clock's pendulum. Click… click… click… click. Within minutes, he dozed off, head slumping to his chest. He awakened with a start as the door opened and Dr. Robertson kindly asked him into his chambers.

As they exchanged warm greetings, Beau observed Dr. Robertson's office. His massive wooden desk was almost completely buried by papers, documents, and books. On the front of his desk rested a carafe of water beaded by condensation, and two glasses. Three walls of the darkly paneled office were covered by books on floor-to-ceiling shelves. A warm, humid breeze occasionally came through the open window. The atmosphere was stuffy and sticky, thick with the smell of old books, old wood, and old pipe tobacco smoke. A buzzing fly and a ticking clock on the mantel were the only sounds heard. Near the window, there was a small round table with two cane-bottomed chairs. The table appeared to function as an auxiliary desk: on it, there were a few papers and letters held in place by a brass paperweight.

Dr. Robertson graciously motioned to Beau to sit down at the table. Both men took their places across from each other in the creaky chairs. Beau noticed that Dr. Robertson's left hand trembled and that he appeared to attempt to mask the tremor by gripping the table with that hand.

Beau hoped he could stay awake in conditions so conducive to sleep.

Dr. Robertson was in his seventh decade. His hair, beard, and bushy eyebrows were white. His face was wrinkled with age and his eyes, framed by wire-rimmed spectacles, reflected an inner joy and seriousness.

He began the conversation.

"Beau, I'm glad you looked me up. I meant it when I said to contact me if you needed me. I hope you're enjoying your first few weeks at Huguenot College."

"Thank you, sir," Beau replied. "I think the college is wonderful. But I am not doing well. I think the problem is me."

"What do you mean, Beau?"

"I think maybe the other students have had a better basic education. And maybe I'm not smart enough. I'm working as hard as I can, but I'm failing three courses."

Dr. Robertson listened carefully and thoughtfully before he responded. "Beau, let me ask you a few questions. Are you taking care of yourself? Are you getting enough sleep? Are you eating right? Is your roommate situation a good one?"

Beau answered honestly. "My roommate could not be better. We get along well. I know I'm not sleeping enough.

I have to study all the time, even into the early morning hours, to try to catch up and learn what I need to learn. I'm ashamed to tell you that I'm so sleepy that I often fall asleep during lectures."

Beau paused here. Then he opened up completely. "Besides, I think I'm homesick. I've never been away from home before. I miss my home."

Dr. Robertson was a wise man and he was an experienced college president. He had heard this story before from countless other students. "Beau, let me first tell you that you are capable and intelligent. You would not be here if you were not. You can do the work. It may be that you have some catching up to do. If so, you will be even with the other students by Christmas break."

Dr. Robertson removed his spectacles, waited a few seconds, and leaned forward. "Regarding your sleep habits—I would recommend to you that you go to class well-rested. Listen attentively and take good notes. Review your notes immediately after class and be sure you understand what you have just heard in lecture. Give yourself a certain amount of time to study and then go to bed by midnight every night, if not before. You will never become a good student if you have not slept properly."

Dr. Robertson sat back and continued with a friendly, smiling expression on his face. "Finally—homesickness. Being homesick is normal. Lots of other students have been homesick here before, and lots of them are now as well. You don't know it because they don't talk about it."

He wanted to give Beau a few moments to think. Besides, he was hot and thirsty. Dr. Robertson stood up, walked to his desk, and grasped the carafe. He offered Beau a glass of water which Beau eagerly accepted. Dr. Robertson poured two glasses and returned to the small table. The tremor of his left hand was accentuated by the rolling water in the glass. He quickly handed Beau the glass from his right hand, placed the other glass on the table, and sat down, again gripping the table with his left hand. He took a sip of water and continued.

"Beau, here is what I predict. By four weeks from now, you will be in a routine. You will be well-rested. You will still miss your home, but you will begin to feel more at home here. And your homesickness will gradually disappear. Besides, in November, we have Parents' Day. Maybe your parents can come visit you then.

"If you continue to have academic problems, see your professors. They are here to teach you, not fail you. They will help you. And I'm always here if you need me."

Beau listened to Dr. Robertson's advice and realized it was wise counsel. He rose from his chair and smiled as he reached out his hand to shake Dr. Robertson's.

"Dr. Robertson, thank you for listening to me and for your advice. I think you are right. I won't give up. I'll make some changes. And I'll see my professors if I need to."

Beau left Dr. Robertson's office feeling better about everything. He began getting the sleep he needed. He studied hard. He asked his professors for help if he didn't understand. He gradually caught up with his peers.

Beau also had something to look forward to; hope is a powerful healer. Parents' Day was coming. And it finally arrived the first Saturday of November. He met his parents at the gates of the college at 10:00 a.m. John and Hannah had brought along a surprise: Grace McLeod. Grace had just turned sixteen, and Beau's parents had given her a birthday gift that had surpassed all the others. They had invited her to accompany them to see Beau when they visited him for Parents' Weekend. They would pay her way. The Soleils knew that both Grace and Beau would love this gift.

Beau hugged his parents and Grace. Grace looked prettier than ever. She wore her best light-blue dress and her long brown hair was shoulder length, tied with a light-blue ribbon.

Beau's heart was full of joy. For the next few hours, he gave them all a tour of the campus. He showed them his lecture halls, classrooms, and laboratories. He introduced them to his friends, some of whom greeted him with, "Good morning, Hammer!" He had become friends with Pete Jones by then after a rocky start, and because of Pete, he knew many of the upperclassmen.

John asked Beau about the nickname. Beau explained how he had earned the name. John felt a secret satisfaction in knowing his son could look out for himself and a blacksmith's pride that his son was known as Hammer.

Thoughtfully, John and Hannah gave Beau and Grace time to be alone. The young couple wandered the campus for several hours after lunch. Beau held Grace's hand as he led her around the grounds. They talked of times in Sure Hope and they talked of times of hope in the future. Much of their time together was spent doing exactly that: savoring time together in silence. Beau knew he would eventually marry Grace. And Grace knew she would marry Beau.

It was finally time for John, Hannah, and Grace to go home. The day had been a healing balm for Beau. He felt a dull, stabbing pain in his chest as he said goodbye, but he knew what it was. He looked forward to going home at Christmas after his exams.

Over time his homesickness magically disappeared.

JUST BEFORE CHRISTMAS BREAK, Mark awakened late one night to Beau's moaning and talking in his sleep. He waited a minute or so for it to subside but the disturbance only worsened. Mark realized that Beau was having a nightmare and recognized the apparent terror in his friend. Mark got out of bed, went to Beau, and shook him. "Beau, you're dreaming. You're having a nightmare. Wake up!" Beau mumbled something Mark could not understand but gradually woke up. Beau was covered in sweat and he was frightened.

"Mark, thank you for waking me up," Beau spoke softly in a low voice. He did not want to awaken other students on their hall. "I was having a nightmare. I have this particular dream that keeps returning. I can't understand it. In the dream I see a young, slender woman. She is wandering in a forest covered in snow. She is carrying something in her arms. And she is sad. I can't ever fully see her face, but I know she's sad. In the dream, I want to help her, but I can't reach her or talk to her. Or she can't hear me. It always ends with my waking up, scared, sweaty, confused, and depressed. I wish I knew what it might mean. I'm sorry to wake you up. You may as well know now that this dream or nightmare keeps coming back. You may have to endure this kind of night again."

Mark told Beau he understood and was sorry for the torment the nightmare caused Beau. He told him not to be concerned for him and that he would keep it between the two of them.

After a few more minutes of conversation, the roommates and friends again went back to sleep.

At unpredictable intervals during their college years, the nightmare returned and they relived the event several more times.

AFTER HIS SECOND YEAR of college, Beau was at the top of his class. He was inducted into Phi Beta Kappa during his junior year. In June 1885, he was graduated from Huguenot College summa cum laude. He had finished all his basic sciences and mathematics, he had learned both Latin and Greek, and he had a good working knowledge of history and literature. He was ready for medical school.

During his college years, he continued his long relationship with Grace McLeod. Their love deepened and they made plans to marry.

9

MEDICAL SCHOOL BEGINS

FROM BEAU'S FIRST DAY at the University School of Medicine in Richmond, he began to learn both the theoretical concepts and the actual practice of medicine. Dr. Barnabas Trust, president of the medical school, welcomed the new students. Dr. Trust was the friend of Beau's physician, Dr. Davis, who had paid Beau a visit after his almost fatal sledding accident. Years before, Dr. Trust had invited Beau to consider becoming a physician and to become a student at the new medical school. The day had finally arrived.

Dr. Trust discussed the curriculum and the culture of medicine. It would be a difficult but fulfilling career and calling, one that required not only intelligence but integrity, perseverance, strength, fortitude, wisdom, curiosity, humility—and compassion. Dr. Trust emphasized to the students the ancient principle: "*Primum, non nocere*. First, do no harm."

Dr. Trust discussed the need to view patients as human beings, not just bodies. He emphasized that humans are made in the image of God and therefore every human is worthy of the best care a physician can give. Physicians, he said, should be physicians of body and soul. Medicine is a calling, not just a job or career, he urged upon the students.

Another of the experienced professors talked about the difference between science and art. "We will teach you the science of medicine," he said. "You will know basic medical science when you graduate. You will begin to learn the art of medicine now but will continue to learn it all your lives. Your patients will teach you much about how to be a physician."

Then, after a brief orientation, professors led Beau and his fellow students into the gross anatomy lab where they would spend many scores of hours learning human anatomy—by dissecting a human cadaver. Entering the lab, they inhaled the distinctive atmosphere of formaldehyde and death, taking care not to breathe too deeply. They gazed with wide eyes as they were instructed to uncover their assigned cadaver. And then they met their cadaver face to face. They attempted to hide their sense of mystery and fear beneath a carefully crafted, self-protective veneer of nonchalance, as if they had done this every day of their lives.

One of the students recognized his cadaver as being

from his home town. Another decided early on that he would avoid dissection as much as possible; he did not want to touch a dead body. He had an aversion to getting his hands messy. He would learn his anatomy from lectures, books, and atlases, he said. (After graduation, he eventually settled into an administrative job, a position where he would not have to touch any patients.) The rest of the students worked together in the careful, meticulous dissection of the upper extremity. Here is where they began, eventually dissecting the entire body.

Beau learned anatomy, and simultaneously, physiology and histology. Still later, he learned pathology. He began to understand why Scripture says that humans are fearfully and wonderfully made.

10

SCOTS PASS: LEARNING BY DOING. A DOG APPEARS

AS PART OF THEIR education, and as a way to serve needy communities, rising third year medical students were assigned to small towns for three months during the summer between their second and third years. Beau Soleil's summer assignment was Scots Pass, Virginia. Scots Pass was a town in the mountains about two hours' ride from Sure Hope. Beau would spend the summer as the town's doctor. He would be all they had.

The people there worked hard, mostly as subsistence farmers or loggers. They were poor. Beau liked being able to help these people because they needed medical care and there was no one else to provide it. He determined to give them the best he had.

Beau would grow to know and love the people of Scots Pass. They would grow to love and trust him.

FROM RICHMOND, after having completed his second-year exams, he traveled home to Sure Hope for a few days and visited his parents. He spent many hours with Grace McLeod. He would live in Scots Pass all summer but would be able to come home every week or two for quick visits. After attending church Sunday morning, Beau packed his doctor's bag, his clothes, and his medical books and mounted his borrowed horse to ride deeper and higher into the Blue Ridge Mountains.

Beau enjoyed riding through the mountain forest. His thoughts wandered. He loved the mountains. No matter what season, he thought, there was the intricate, exquisite beauty of God's creation all around him. In the summer, he loved the smell of the mountain grass and the rhododendron, and the cool of the green, leafy, shady mountain terrain. He drank from the swiftly running cold streams, and if he got hot, he swam in them. In the fall, he was overwhelmed with the explosion of color as the leaves turned to deep red and orange and yellow; the sun on the leaves made them appear like a painter's palette. Winters made travel more difficult, but what is more breathtaking than a white blanket of snow on smooth, sloping mountain shoulders, much like a white shawl on a beautiful woman? The muffled sounds in the quiet of deep midwinter gave him a sense of inner peace and joy, a knowledge that being still and knowing God was enough. And the springtime, with its freshness and light-green leaves, all the earth reminding us that, yes, there is a time of newness to come, a time when all will be made right—who can deny the power of new life?

The ride to Scots Pass gave him two hours of precious solitude, two hours to think, two hours to be with the God he loved and to drink in the work of God's hands. He thought, "God is such a God of goodness, of variety, of diversity. He is the ultimate artist and engineer. God could have made everything from a strictly functional and utilitarian point of view, and it would have worked. But God is always better than he needs to be or than we expect him to be: he crowns our lives with beauty, not just function."

The day was getting hot as Beau arrived in Scots Pass. Mr. and Mrs. Johnson, unofficial but recognized leaders in the town, met him at their home and then showed him to his room and office. There was a small house downtown that the residents of Scots Pass had converted for the use of their assigned medical student each summer. The house contained basic medical supplies and a comfortable room for Beau's lodging. Back at the Johnsons' home, Mrs. Johnson gave him some refreshment, and Mr. Johnson gave him a list of the sick patients he needed to visit on his rounds the next day. Thanking the Johnsons, Beau returned to his new home, unpacked and arranged his clothes, books, and equipment, and went to bed early. He planned to begin his rounds on Monday before the sun came up.

HE ARRIVED MONDAY MORNING at the home of William and Sarah Blair to check on Sarah and her one-week-old baby, Simeon. Sarah was doing fine, felt well, and was enjoying being a mother for the first time. She had no signs of infection and William saw to it that his wife was resting as she needed to. Sarah's mother was living with them for a couple of weeks to help out. Baby Simeon appeared to be thriving and he liked to eat. He knew what he was supposed to do, and he was well on track to eventually becoming as big as his father, a powerfully built man, a logger whose strength was well known among the mountain folk.

Next, Beau stopped at the home of Joanna Green. Joanna was a five-year-old girl with a bad rash. He rode into view of the house and Mrs. Green greeted him. "Mr. Soleil, welcome. It's good to have you here this summer. Thank you for coming today. My daughter has had a rash for a few days. She's itching something terrible and can't stop scratching."

Beau entered the house and saw a pretty little girl with brown hair playing on the floor. She looked up as he came in. Her face was covered in a red rash and lines of blisters. She scratched her face as she played.

"Hello, Joanna. I'm Beau Soleil. How are you feeling?" Beau smiled at her and approached her slowly.

"I feel fine, Doctor. But I have this rash and it itches. Bad. Real bad."

"Joanna, can you show me where you have your rash?"

Mrs. Green helped Joanna show the doctor the rash on her face, neck, hands, and arms. The rash was red, raised, and linear. There were blisters; some of them had popped and were oozing. There were scratch marks everywhere the rash occurred. The rash was only on exposed areas of skin. There was no rash in the areas protected by clothing.

"Joanna, do you like to play in the woods?" Beau asked the question, but he knew the answer.

"I love to play in the woods. I go there every day. I'm making a house in the woods for my dolls."

"Joanna, when was the last time you went into the woods? And Mrs. Green, when did the rash appear?" Beau was taking a careful history to prove the diagnosis to himself.

"Mr. Soleil, Joanna was last in the woods about four days ago." Mrs. Green took over and answered for both of them. "The rash began two days ago. It started red and itchy and now it is red and itchy and blistery."

"Mrs. Green, Joanna has poison oak or poison sumac. It's not serious. I'm sure she brushed it in the woods, or touched a leaf or vine with her hands. She spread it to her face with her hands. It's only on areas of exposed skin. Her clothing protected her. The rash will go away in a few days but it *does* itch. Do you have any calamine lotion? I think I have some in my bag if you don't."

Mrs. Green told him that she had some calamine. Beau left instructions to use cool, wet compresses several times a day on the rash, then to allow the skin to dry, and then apply calamine lotion. He gave Joanna a piece of hard candy, patted her on the arm, and told her to be careful in the woods. He asked her mother to show Joanna what poison sumac and poison oak looked like so she could avoid it later.

Just as he was leaving, Mrs. Green stopped Beau with a question. "Dr. Soleil, do you mind if I ask you to look at another of my daughters? I hadn't planned on asking, but I need your help if you have time."

Beau told her he had time to stay a little longer. "What kind of problem is she having, Mrs. Green?"

"Well, Stella is my two-year-old. She is sweet and no trouble at all. See her over there?" Stella was as pretty as her big sister, her brown hair falling in ringlets around her chubby pink face. She was playing in the corner with a doll.

"I'm embarrassed to tell you this, Doctor. But Stella smells. Really bad. So bad that no one can stand to be near her. Her older brother has taken to calling her Stinky instead of Stella."

Beau had noticed a terrible odor as he entered the home thirty minutes before. He had tried to ignore it. He had wondered if it was his imagination. Or maybe there was something dead near the house. He politely had not mentioned it. But now that the subject was brought up, he pursued it.

"Mrs. Green, how long have you noticed this smell?"

"I first noticed it about three weeks ago. Stella has not been sick. She is playing normally. She has had a runny nose but no cough or fever. She just stinks. Bad. She is clean. I bathe her a few times every week. Her clothes are clean. I'm a good mother. I take care of my children. But as much as I love her, the smell has gotten so bad I can barely stand to kiss her!"

Beau looked over at the little cherub and wondered what was wrong. She appeared healthy. He asked her mother to bring Stella over to him. He had situated himself near a window in order to have the light he needed to examine her. The closer Stella got, the more intense the smell became. Her mother had not exaggerated.

Beau began by playing with her a little. He asked to see her rag doll and noticed it had a hole in the side; some of the cotton stuffing was coming out. "Stella, hello. What is your baby's name?"

"Baby." As Stella spoke, the air was filled with her breath, and it was not the sweet breath of a baby. No. Not at all.

"Stella, can you open your mouth for me? Like this?" Beau showed her how to do it and she imitated him. Beau attempted to hold his breath as he looked at her teeth, gums, and throat. She looked normal.

"Mrs. Green, please tell me again when you noticed the smell and the runny nose."

"It all began about three weeks ago."

Beau noticed that only one nostril was draining. And draining it was: a thick, green, putrid, malodorous discharge was coming from her left nostril and running onto her upper lip.

Beau gently tilted Stella's head back and allowed the sun streaming through the window to light his way. He was repulsed by the incredible stench coming from this sweet little girl. He noticed what he thought was a fibrous substance in her left nostril.

Reaching into his bag, Beau pulled out some forceps. He asked Mrs. Green to hold Stella's head and he explained to Stella what he was about to do. He assured her it would not hurt.

Quickly and deftly, Beau grasped the fibrous matter at the center of the green gunk and withdrew from her nose a one-inch-long cylindrical mass of cotton, gooey green mucus, and decaying debris. The smell was the worst he had ever experienced. He thought he was going to vomit. Beau walked to the doorway and flung the mass into the woods.

Returning to his patient and her mother, Beau told them triumphantly, "I think your problem is solved. Stella will smell normal within a day or so. She's cured."

The mystery of the stench was no longer a mystery. It became apparent that when Stella had been playing quietly over the past few weeks, she had been removing stuffing from Baby and stuffing her own nose. And only her left nostril. She was left-handed.

The grateful mother gave Beau a fresh loaf of bread as he left. Medicine has its rewards.

THE NEXT HOME HE visited was that of Mrs. Odie Grouse. Her given name was Euodia, but for several reasons, her family and friends called her Odie. Behind her back, some called her Odious.

Mrs. Odie Grouse had a myriad of complaints—always. In Richmond, Beau had been warned about her from the previous medical student. The Johnsons had repeated the warning just as he had arrived in Scots Pass. Mrs. Grouse had a reputation. She was a sad and lonely woman whose husband had left her a widow many years ago and whose children had long since left the area. Mrs. Grouse was an exacting and demanding woman; she had great difficulty forgiving any slight, any offense, or any failure to meet her expectations. As a result, she had become more and more bitter about her life. People were always disappointing her.

She was angry with God, she was angry with her family, she was angry with just about everyone in Scots Pass, and she was angry with herself. She was even angry with her deceased husband for having died. Beau approached her home with a mixture of sadness and frustration—sadness because he felt sorry for her, and frustration because he worried that her list of symptoms would overwhelm his (or anyone's) abilities and time to remedy them. He thought he would have little to offer her.

He remembered and reminded himself of some important lessons he had been taught in medical school. Always listen carefully to a patient. Always take a patient seriously. Always begin a patient encounter with an open mind. Never assume that the patient continues with the same diagnosis. Never neglect taking a full history and doing a complete physical exam. Things change. Patients change. New diseases arise.

He took a deep breath, feeling guilty that he really didn't want to deal with her today, and realizing he should want to help her no matter how difficult or frustrating she might be. He braced himself as he knocked on the door and was invited into the front room. His patient was a middle-aged woman with graying hair. She did not appear to be very ill. The woman did not rise to meet him but asked him to sit down.

Beau introduced himself with a smile. "Good morning,

Mrs. Grouse, I'm Beau Soleil, the new medical student. I understand you have not been feeling well lately."

Mrs. Grouse moaned as she talked. "I've been expecting you, Mr. Soleil. Good morning. I mean—what's good about it? I didn't sleep a wink last night. I feel exhausted this morning and I've been weak for months. My knees hurt me, and I've had headaches every day for the past three years. My stomach hurts all the time. Also, I feel dizzy when I stand up. And my chest hurts. My heart beats fast. I have a lot of problems. And I'm also really upset with my neighbor. Do you know that Mrs. Dora Morrison—she's my neighbor— Mrs. Morrison forgot my birthday? How could she? I never forget hers. My children are all grown and never visit me. They say they're busy. Busy? I was never too busy for them. And my dearly departed husband—he died and departed. Besides, he was lazy. He wanted to stop working every day when the sun went down. He only wanted to work from sunup to sundown. Not me. A woman's work is never done. I'm not lazy. Well, my dearly departed husband left when he died. Can you believe that? How could he? When I needed him the most. He just up and died. He was so selfish. So now I'm alone, to face the slings and arrows of the world by myself. Doctor—may I call you Doctor?—can you help me? Please, I need help. I'm suffering, Doctor. Is there some medicine you can give me? Something? Please?" Mrs. Grouse finally stopped to catch her breath after this torrent of words. She seemed exhausted from talking nonstop.

Beau broke into the conversation when he had the chance. He had listened to her talk, listened intently and patiently. He could not shape her constellation of symptoms into a unifying diagnosis. He asked a few clarifying questions. He concluded: "Mrs. Grouse, I'm sorry it has been so difficult for you and I'm sorry you're feeling so poorly. Do you mind if I examine you?"

With her assent, he performed a physical examination. Her exam was completely normal. She did not have a goiter, she had a normal heart and lung exam, and her abdominal exam revealed no tumors. She had no swelling of her legs. Her nail beds and mucous membranes were pink; she did not appear to be anemic.

"Mrs. Grouse, I'm happy to tell you that your exam is normal. I do not think you have any type of serious disease. You are getting a little older, as everyone does. But I think you are healthy." Beau attempted to reassure her and to demonstrate that he cared about her.

Mrs. Grouse seemed to relax. She seemed to be at ease. She knew Beau had taken the time to listen to her and to try to understand her. "Doctor, thank you for being so careful today. I feel better just knowing I have nothing serious. What do you think is wrong with me?"

Beau thought carefully but quickly before he

answered. The symptoms were too numerous, too vague, and too unconnected to fit a nice, clear-cut diagnosis. Her exam was normal. She *was* a difficult woman; she was her own worst enemy (aren't we all?). She was in pain and she was suffering. Her pain was real, but it was an inner pain that expressed itself in what she thought was the more acceptable, less humiliating (she thought) pain of the body. Her bodily complaints were the result of her real inner pain. She was crying out for someone to help her. Beau knew that what she needed most was a change that would allow her to forgive others and allow her to give up her anger and bitterness. In addition, she needed someone to talk to, someone who would listen. She needed to unburden herself of her inner pain, and calling the young medical student for help was the only way she knew to acceptably ask for it. He hoped he could help her as their relationship deepened over the summer. But now was not the time to attempt to undo what years had done.

He finally answered. "Mrs. Grouse, I think your body is healthy. I want to reassure you of that. You have suffered much in your life. God understands our suffering and he is not at a distance watching. He is with us even in our suffering. I think you are going to have a good week. I plan to come back to check on you next week." Beau prayed that a little kindness and understanding might have a good effect. He offered her hope.

As Beau gathered his instruments and repacked his medical bag, Mrs. Grouse smiled, just a little. She seemed more cheerful. "Thank you for coming, Doctor. Thank you."

Beau would return to see Mrs. Euodia Grouse on multiple occasions that summer.

DURING HIS SUMMER IN Scots Pass, Beau's routine remained fairly constant. He arose early and he arrived at his first house call by 8:00 a.m. He saw most of his patients in their homes. Most illnesses were routine. Beau Soleil grew in expertise and confidence as the summer stretched into July and August, and the people of Scots Pass grew to appreciate their young medical student as he matured.

Young Jimmy McIntosh was a seven-year-old boy with bright red hair and freckles and a toothless smile. He loved to roam the woods, and a few days ago had scraped his thigh while climbing a tree. The area had become swollen and red, and now it was extremely painful. His parents had sent word to Beau to look at their son's "risin'." Beau greeted Jimmy and his parents with a cheerful "hello" and went to work. He felt the three-by-three-inch area of swelling and it was exquisitely tender and red. The overlying skin was thinned out and shiny, and it felt fluctuant (squishy). Jimmy had a boil. The cure was easy, but it would hurt. Beau explained to Jimmy what he would have to do, taking great care to be honest, yet not scare him. With his back to Jimmy to screen what he was doing, Beau reached for his bag and pulled out a scalpel. He held the blade over an open flame until it was bright red, then poured alcohol over it. He turned around and wiped Jimmy's skin off with alcohol. He instructed Jimmy not to touch the cleansed skin and not to reach for Beau's hands. He told Jimmy to squeeze his mother's hands hard and to take three deep breaths. On the third breath, Beau plunged the knife blade into the abscess, followed by the insertion of small hemostats into the wound to open it up. There was a gush of bloody, thick pus that almost squirted onto Beau's shirt. It smelled horrible. The boil was drained and Jimmy was cured.

ONE DAY, HE RECEIVED a message to come to the home of Josiah Outlaw. One of the Outlaw children was ill. Beau rode up to a rude but neat log cabin and a boy of about fifteen greeted him.

"Good morning, son. I'm Beau Soleil. Is Mr. Outlaw here? I have a note from him asking me to come see Zeke."

The boy answered, "Hello, Mister. I'm Josiah Outlaw. There ain't no Mr. or Mrs. Outlaw here." As he spoke, a little girl came into the doorway and joined Josiah. The girl appeared to be about three years old.

"I don't understand, Josiah. Where are your parents?"

"Our parents died two years ago when our house done

burned down. It was in January and we was all a-sleepin'. It was a cold night and it was a-snowin'. We had built the fire up afore we went to bed. About two in the mornin', the chimney caught fire. Our parents both died in the fire. Two of our brothers died. We survived because our father and mother kept a-goin' back into the house to find us and rescue us. We lost our parents and our brothers. We lost our house and everything we owned. Only three of us made it."

Beau listened to the story and allowed Josiah to go on.

"This here's Eunice. Eunice was too young then to remember anything about the fire. But not Zeke. He was four years old then. He's six now. He remembers everything. Everything. When the fire done burned out and there was nothin' but smoke and smolderin' ashes, he went back into the house. He found our parents' burned bodies. When he saw them, he fell on 'em and hugged 'em. He began a-cryin' and a-weepin' and a-wailin'. I finally went in and pulled him off of 'em. He ain't been normal since. He stopped talkin' then and he still cain't talk. He don't never smile."

Beau fought back his tears. He asked the obvious question. "Josiah, do you mean to tell me that you are the head of this house now? How do you make it?"

"Doctor, when our house burned down, neighbors come to help us. They was good to us. They brung us food, they done built us a new cabin, and they give us some feed and a few livestock. I was thirteen years old then and told 'em we wanted to stay together. We wanted to live here. We stayed. Me—I take good care of the young'uns. Our nearest neighbors, the Lewises, are always a-helpin' us and a-checkin' on us. I'm a good shot with my rifle and shoot squirrels and rabbits for us to eat. Once in a while, I shoot a deer. I catch lots of fish. We make it."

Beau shook his head, amazed that this young boy could care for his siblings and himself as he was doing. He identified with these children as orphans. He wondered how he would have done in this situation.

"Josiah, you have done well. I want to spend more time with you this summer to see if I can help you. But, for now, let's take a look at Zeke. Can you please tell me what is wrong with him now?"

"Zeke is in bed sick. He's bad sick. Bad sick. He had a sore throat a little bit ago. Then, a few days ago, he started a-havin' blood when he makes water. He acts like his haid hurts. He won't get outta bed."

Josiah walked Beau to the bed in the main room and they found Zeke lying there, groaning. He had his hands held to his head as if in pain and he was crying off and on. Beau placed his hand on Zeke's forehead, both stroking his hair and feeling for fever; he was not hot. Beau spoke in low and soothing tones in an attempt to comfort Zeke. Zeke never answered Beau, but his words had a calming effect on the suffering and frightened boy. Beau kept talking and explained to Zeke that he needed to look at him. As Beau withdrew the covers, he noticed that Zeke had swollen legs and a swollen abdomen. He had pitting edema over his shins.

Beau asked if Josiah had saved any of Zeke's urine. Josiah produced a glass jar full of fluid. Beau walked to a window and held the jar up to the light. The fluid was a smoky, reddish color.

Beau knew that Zeke had nephritis.

"Josiah, your brother has a kidney problem. It will probably get better over the next few days. Zeke should start to feel better soon, his headache will gradually disappear, and his water will begin to clear. The leg swelling will get better also.

"For now, get Zeke to eat whatever he can. But—he needs to stay away from anything salty. He should not have ham or sausage or any salted meat. Give him water to drink but not too much.

"I will come back to check on him in a few days. If he gets worse, call for me."

"Thank you, Doc. I feel better about my little brother. I cain't pay you today, but I'll pay you sho'nuf as soon as I sell a few deerskins." Josiah was relieved.

"Josiah, I won't charge you anything. Save your money. I want to do this for free." Beau wanted the family to save their resources.

Before he left, Beau knelt by Zeke's bedside, placed his hand on his head, bent over his ear and whispered to him, "Zeke, you will be alright. I'll check on you in a few days." Zeke seemed to relax as he spoke the calming words.

When Beau returned three days later, Zeke was walking around, not playing yet, but feeling much better. His swelling was down and the blood in his urine was almost gone.

Zeke recovered from the nephritis, but he never recovered his ability to speak. He rarely smiled. Beau had many long conversations with Josiah that summer. Beau made certain that the Lewises and others in town continued to watch out for the Outlaws. And Josiah kept the household going.

EARLY ONE COOL SUMMER MORNING, Beau stepped out of his front door in Scots Pass and prepared to make his mountain rounds. He mounted his horse and slowly meandered to the edge of town. He was still a little drowsy after a long night. He had been called to perform a difficult delivery during the early hours of the morning. The delivery had been successful: both mother and babe were fine. Beau had returned home for a couple of hours of sleep. He was tired now.

As he left the outskirts of town, he noticed out of the corner of his eye that something small was moving, just slightly, in the woods. He ignored it at first, thinking it must be a squirrel or bird. Or maybe a rabbit? He *tried* to ignore it and just move on. Besides, he was too tired to care. However, his curiosity won out. The gravitational pull of the object drew him closer and he saw on the ground a small furry ball.

Beau dismounted and slowly walked into the woods. He knelt on the pine-straw-covered forest floor. There in front of him was a little gray puppy. He was mostly fur. Beau picked the little dog up and held him in his hand to inspect him more closely. The dog was not much bigger than Beau's palm.

Beau looked around to find the dog's mother. After a thorough search of the surrounding woods, no mother was found. There were no other puppies nearby. Beau wondered what had happened. Had the mother been killed by a predator? Had someone discarded this puppy in the woods? It was impossible to tell. Only a couple of things were apparent: Beau held a pretty little puppy in his hand, and Beau had a decision to make.

The Soleil family dog, Amos, had died a few years ago. Beau missed having a dog around. The puppy looked into Beau's eyes with a mixture of hope, expectation, gratitude, and love. Beau could not resist. Again, the pull of gravity was too great for him. He made his decision. He gently placed the little dog in his side coat pocket and took him home.

Once inside his house, Beau poured a little milk into a bowl and watched the puppy lap it up. Beau found an old blanket and made a bed on the floor for his new companion. He placed some outdated newspapers on the floor under the dog's bed and around it and hoped for the best.

Beau needed to name his new dog. He thought calling him Amos might be confusing. Canine or K9 seemed a little pretentious. And calling him Dog seemed ridiculous. Beau studied him carefully as his new friend finished his milk and then, as if trained, burrowed into the old blanket and went to sleep.

The dog was a grayish color. His face was slightly wolf-like. He might become a big dog someday. He might not. He seemed to be a mixed breed; it was impossible to tell much now about his future size.

Beau decided his new puppy would be called Wolf. If the pup grew to become a large dog with wolf-like features, Beau's name for him would prove to be well chosen and prophetic. There was also the possible benefit that Beau could boast that his dog was actually part wolf.

If the puppy wound up little when fully grown, the name Wolf would seem ironic and Beau could say the name was a joke. Besides, if he were small, the name Wolf might inform what Beau hoped would be the dog's feisty personality, full of courage and heart.

Time would tell. But for now, Beau had a dog. And Wolf had a man.

OVER THE NEXT MONTHS, Wolf grew into his destiny and his name. His coat remained gray. His face became ever more lupine in appearance and his body filled out—a lot. He consumed an immense amount of food; he also destroyed many shirts, coats, trousers, shoes, and table legs in his first years of life. By the time he was fully grown, he weighed a muscular ninety pounds. He was gently affectionate toward his master and fiercely protective of him. When Wolf snarled and bared his teeth toward an enemy, real or perceived, he made his point. On occasions without number over the ensuing years, Beau heard entreaties for mercy from panicked strangers, strangers that Wolf viewed as threats he needed to neutralize. The pleas were always some variant of: "Please, Mister, call your dog off! Please!!"

Beau also heard a common question from the same mouths of those who had the fear of Wolf in their eyes: "Mister—does he bite?" To this question, Beau had a complete repertoire of answers. He might say to the frightened innocent, "No, my dog might be named Wolf, but he should have been named Lamb. He won't bite you. He never bites." This was his usual answer. Wolf, in fact, did not bite humans. But his bark and snarl were fearsome.

To the obvious miscreant who was cowering in fear before Wolf, Beau had another answer to the "does he bite?" query. Beau might say, matter-of-factly, "Friend, my dog is named Wolf. He's named Wolf for a reason. I have no control over what Wolf might do."

And to the person whose character seemed dubious and whose intentions were not clear, Beau might say something confusing. "I'm not sure what my dog will do. What do *you* think?" And to still others, he might answer more cryptically, "My dog bites only those he doesn't like." Beau's answers to this pressing question depended on the person and the situation.

Wolf became a beloved friend and companion. He was devoted and loyal to his master as only a dog can be. He provided comfort and company for Beau. Wolf was a sheep in wolf's clothing.

11

MEDICAL SCHOOL WRAPS UP. THE NEXT ADVENTURE

FOR THREE YEARS, BEAU devoted his time and energy to learning all he could of the basic sciences and then, gradually, the art of medicine, following his professors and working with them as they cared for their patients. Beau realized that anything he could learn could be important to the care of his future patients. Thus, he read textbooks and journals. He attended lectures. He questioned his professors. He wanted to understand. He learned to think like a physician.

Beau learned to empathize with his suffering patients. He learned to discipline himself so that he did not reveal his fear or let fear master him as he entered life and death situations. He learned to endure blood, horrific stench, and sickening trauma. He learned to function and maintain his equanimity in the middle of aggressive assault on all his senses. He learned to master his emotions while still keeping them alive.

During this time, Beau continued in his meticulous ways. He learned to pay attention to details, whether in interviewing patients or in following their disease course. He disciplined himself to hone his powers of observation and to utilize all his senses in caring for patients. By the time of his graduation in 1888, Beau was comfortable with seeing patients, taking a good history and performing a thorough physical examination, diagnosing most diseases, and prescribing medications. He was a moderately adept surgeon.

During his third year of medical school, Beau came across some verses in the Gospel of St. Luke that forever impacted his practice of medicine. He loved to read Luke because Luke was a physician. Luke wrote like a physician. He observed with care and wrote descriptions with detail. He described medical diseases as only a physician could.

Luke 9:2 arrested Beau's attention early one morning:

And he sent them to preach the kingdom of God, and to heal the sick.

Beau's mind immediately went to Matthew 4:23:

And Jesus went about all Galilee, teaching in their synagogues, and preaching the gospel of the kingdom, and healing all manner of sickness and all manner of disease among the people.

Beau realized that just as Jesus had preached the gospel and healed people, he had commissioned his disciples to proclaim the kingdom and heal the sick. And he knew that just as surely, he, as a Christian physician, wanted to do the same thing: share the gospel and heal people. He knew he could not really heal people. Only God can heal. But he also knew that God could use him as an instrument of healing.

Everyone needs healing.

Beau was also learning from experience that patients often share with their physician much more than physical complaints. They often confide in their doctors, sharing intimate relational details or inner struggles or deep emotional wounds.

And at about this same time, Beau discovered the writings of Dr. Thomas Sydenham, the famous Christian physician of the 1600s known as the English Hippocrates. In addition to his pioneering work in clinical medicine and epidemiology, Dr. Sydenham had thought deeply about what it took to become a fine physician, and had articulated his ideas with clarity and precision in a written record.

Said Thomas Sydenham:

It becomes every man who purposes to give himself to the care of others, seriously to consider the four following things:

First, that he must one day give an account to the Supreme Judge of all the lives entrusted to his care.

Secondly, that all his skill, and knowledge, and energy as they have been given him by God, so they should be exercised for his glory, and the good of mankind, and not for mere gain or ambition.

Thirdly, and not more beautifully than truly, let him reflect that he has undertaken the care of no mean creature, for, in order that he may estimate the value, the greatness of the human race, the only begotten Son of God became himself a man, and thus ennobled it with his divine dignity, and far more than this, died to redeem it.

And fourthly, that the doctor being himself a mortal man, should be diligent and tender in relieving his suffering patients, inasmuch as he himself must one day be a like sufferer.

Beau's thoughts about the essence of being a true physician began to crystallize. Beau resolved, with God's help, to become a truly Christian physician. He would ask God to use him in physical healing. He would also ask God to use him to apply the healing gospel of Jesus Christ as the opportunity arose. Everyone needs a Savior. Everyone needs healing. Everyone needs forgiveness of sin. Everyone needs redemption.

Beau's view of the true nature of medical practice was forever changed, and this view shaped his care of patients throughout his entire career.

BEAU THOUGHT HE NEEDED more training before he could give the high quality care he wanted to offer the people of Sure Hope. He asked his patron and friend, Mr. Argenta, for a one-year extension before he returned home to practice, and Mr. Argenta readily agreed. They trusted each other and shook hands on their agreement. After finishing medical school, then, Beau spent the month of June in Sure Hope before traveling to his next step of training: Philadelphia, a major center of American medical education and innovation.

In Sure Hope, Beau spent time with his parents, helped Dr. Davis in his still busy practice, and lived to enjoy Grace's presence. Beau loved Grace with all his heart. She understood him. She knew how to delve into the deep areas of his soul to help him understand himself. She knew how to encourage him when he despaired. She knew his moods. Grace forgave his anger and impatience. Grace knew that Beau was a man who, above all else, desired to glorify and please God. Yet, she also knew that he attempted to carry too much on his own shoulders. Grace was fiercely loyal to Beau. She was also courageous enough to tell him the truth when he was wrong. Beau needed her. He needed her beauty, her gentleness, and her wisdom. He needed her love.

Grace and Beau took long walks in the forest and along the banks of the river. They often took a picnic basket and arranged to spend an entire day away from others. And they talked of their future together. They both dreaded the day fast approaching when Beau would leave for Philadelphia for one more year of training. It was a long trip from Sure Hope to Philadelphia and they knew they would hardly see each other during that time.

THE DAY OF BEAU'S DEPARTURE rushed toward Grace and Beau like a locomotive and then arrived. The night before he left, Beau had dinner at the McLeods' home. Afterwards, Grace and Beau went for a walk in the cool of the mountain evening, night settling over the town. Beau took Grace's hand and led her to their favorite west-facing overlook; they watched a glorious sunset together one last time. Beau put his arm around Grace's waist, drew her close, and kissed her. From his pocket, he produced a small package and handed it to Grace. She carefully tore the white paper, opened the box, and gasped with joy as she adored the small golden heart pendant Beau had bought for her.

"Grace," Beau spoke with love and tenderness, "this is a reminder of me. Don't forget me. Wait for me. I'll be back for you. I'm going to marry you someday, Grace McLeod. I love you."

Beau helped Grace fasten the pendant around her neck and she reached up to Beau, placing her arms around his neck. They again kissed. Grace had tears in her eyes now as she realized how much she loved Beau and how much she would miss him. Just after midnight, they walked back to town.

BEAU LEFT SURE HOPE five hours later for Philadelphia.

12

THE EPIDEMIC

BEAU SOLEIL FINISHED HIS work at the hospital as he made rounds on his last few patients. They would be fine until he saw them again the next morning, he thought. He was exhausted after having worked fourteen hours.

There was an epidemic ravaging the city of Philadelphia. From what he had heard, the same illness was spreading all along the eastern seaboard. From medical protocols inherited from the 1600s in Venice, Italy and the 1700s in Austria-Hungary, sick or exposed residents of the City of Brotherly Love were quarantined in an effort to stem the spread of disease. Yet the illness continued to rage. Hundreds died from the sickness, especially the very young, the very old, and those with chronic diseases.

Beau and his fellow physicians were overworked and under-rested.

Early that morning, Beau had been urgently awakened by a runner from the hospital because a woman was in severe respiratory distress. She was the patient of another physician, a senior attending doctor. The woman was known to have pneumonia, a pneumonia they saw commonly as a complication of the illness in the community. The woman had suddenly decompensated. When Beau arrived at her bedside, the elderly woman could barely speak because she could barely breathe; her skin color was bluish, and she was semiconscious. He listened to her lungs and noticed decreased, almost absent breath sounds on the left. He percussed her thorax and noted dullness on the same side. Her trachea was deviated to the right. From the physical findings, Beau knew that she had a pleural effusion or empyema (fluid or pus in her pleural space, the area surrounding her lungs). He also knew what he had to do. Unless he acted promptly, she would die. A nurse washed the woman's back with soap and water. She then wiped the skin with alcohol. Beau found a large gauge needle, a syringe with a three-way stopcock, and rubber tubing. He placed the needle between the ribs on her back, punctured the skin and muscle just over a rib until the needle tip arrived in the pleural space, and withdrew a syringe full of thick, cloudy fluid. He emptied the fluid into a metal basin. He repeated the process ten times, thus drawing off a large quantity of the foul-smelling, purulent fluid. The woman began to breathe more easily as her lung volume was restored. Her color improved.

The thoracentesis had worked.

This was but one of the many life-saving procedures he had learned since having arrived in Philadelphia a few months before. After medical school, he had wanted an extra year of training by some of the best physicians in the world: Philadelphia was the place to be. He knew the additional year of education would ultimately benefit his future patients in Sure Hope, Virginia.

As HE LEFT THE hospital and stepped outside into the cold Philadelphia evening, he was tired but he was happy. Snow lay in drifts all around, but the sky was clear and the February air was crisp. Beau was glad to have his heavy overcoat and hat. He was also glad to be able to walk a few blocks to Mrs. Harrison's house where he rented a room. The walk home always refreshed him and helped clear his mind.

He missed his home in Sure Hope and he missed Grace. His training in Philadelphia would be over in a few months and he would return home for good. Then he would wed his Gracie.

Sweet Mrs. Harrison warmly met Beau at the door as he entered and she informed him that dinner would be served in twenty minutes. He was hungry and did not need her to tell him dinner was almost ready: the aroma had greeted him before Mrs. Harrison had. Mrs. Harrison's motherly instincts told her he was exhausted. Beau's slumped shoulders and the dark circles beneath his eyes betrayed him despite his efforts to hide his fatigue. She handed him a letter that had arrived a few hours before. Beau recognized the flowing handwriting and could not keep himself from unconsciously raising the envelope to his face to enjoy the delicious scent of perfume. The letter was from Grace. He thanked Mrs. Harrison and quickly ascended the stairs to his garret room where he opened the welcome letter. He sat on the edge of his bed to read it but not before again luxuriating in the olfactory reminder of his Gracie.

On the envelope was this address:

Dr. Beau Soleil
Care of Mrs. Harrison
237 Chestnut Street
Philadelphia, Pennsylvania

Beau smiled. Grace loved to call him "Dr. Soleil." He was glad she was proud of him. And he loved to receive her letters. He always read and re-read them, then saved them for later reading. He wanted to enjoy all the pleasure he could gather from her letters. He loved her flowing cursive script, uncorrupted as his had been by the rushed hospital environment. He loved the blue ink. He loved the perfumed paper. Grace's letters helped Beau to remember who he was and why he did what he did.

He unfolded the letter.

February 6, 1889

Dear Beau,

I miss you, Beau. Please come home.

There is a sickness going through Sure Hope that is killing people. No one knows what it is, but babies, young children, and old people are dying. Almost everyone is catching it. It begins with fever, coughing, sore throat, and muscle aches and pains. It lasts about five days and then most recover slowly. But some never get well and then they die.

Your mother began to be sick a week ago. We thought she was getting better but then she started to run a fever again and developed a terrible cough. Dr. Davis said she had pneumonia. I have been with her the past two days nursing her and trying to keep her comfortable. Dr. Davis has been by several times a day as he made his daily house calls to the sick people in town. Your mother grew worse and worse. There was finally nothing Dr. Davis could do for her. Beau, your mother is with the Lord.

I wish I could be there to tell you face to face. I loved your mother and I love you. Your father is full of grief and sadness.

Please come home. We need you. The funeral will be in a few days.

I am sorry to write you with this bad news.

I love you.

Your Grace

The letter dropped from his hand and floated to the floor. His head dropped into his hands and a torrent of tears rolled down his cheeks as if a great seawall had burst. The sorrow was suffocating. Grief and guilt and gratitude rolled over him like great waves in a stormy sea. He felt he could not breathe and he felt nauseated. Here he was in Philadelphia helping to save the lives of others. Yet his mother had died of the same thing he had saved a woman from just a few hours earlier. If he had been in Sure Hope, could he have prevented his mother's death? Had she needed a thoracentesis? He thought of all the unresolvable questions and possibilities. Why had he even come to Philadelphia? He felt guilty for ever having left Sure Hope.

His mother had adopted him and loved him. She had taught him the Bible and how to pray. She had led him to Jesus Christ. She had bandaged his wounds. She had always believed in him. She had suffered for him.

There is a certain mysterious and precious quality that God places in women and girls, deeper and stronger than men possess: It is an extraordinary capacity, an inner reserve of strength, to serve and sacrifice and suffer for the ones they love, never complaining, never even noticing. They expect nothing in return. They are faithful even to those who do not deserve it. It is all love.

Beau thought, "Why Mama? Why not someone else? *Anybody* else? Why not me?"

He loved his mother. He would miss her. He was grateful for her. And he could not explain or answer all the questions he had. Then the thought came to him: God knows. I can trust him. He knows the way that I take. "The Lord giveth and the Lord taketh away. Blessed be the name of the Lord." He remembered that the Lord is near the brokenhearted, applying the healing balm of his grace and love.

Beau could not eat dinner. He told Mrs. Harrison what had happened and, eyes full of tears, she gently hugged him and whispered words of consolation. He sent word to the hospital that he must return to his home immediately, then packed his luggage, hired a carriage to take him to the train station, and caught the last train to Washington, D.C. He dozed fitfully in his upright seat. He dreamt of home and slept in a strange mixture of peace and anxiety and terror, the peace being interrupted by nightmares of dying patients he had just left. And the recurring dream came back again. He dreamed again of a thin young woman wandering in deep darkness through snowy woods. He could never fully see her face, but he could see enough to know that she bore a sad and despairing expression. In her arms she carried a mysterious bundle. And her wandering seemed aimless and endless. He never understood this dream (or was it a vision?). Why did it keep coming back? What did it mean? But each time the dream occurred, he awoke with a start and felt a shroud of great sadness enveloping him, so real he could almost touch it. For an hour, he was unable to return to sleep as he pondered the meaning of the dream. He finally drifted off again for a short time.

At about 5 a.m. he awakened for good with an unsettling blend of joy, anxiety, sadness, and confusion. The train arrived in Washington at about six o'clock. Beau ate a small breakfast in the station and then boarded the train to Winchester. From there, it was a short stagecoach ride to Sure Hope.

BEAU WALKED INTO HIS home just after noon and met John Soleil as he came out the front door. Father and son fell into each other's arms and sobbed. It was good to feel his father's strong blacksmith arms again. John had always been a refuge of quiet, gentle strength for Beau. For a brief moment, Beau felt like a five-year-old boy again.

"Daddy, I am so sorry for you, and so sorry for both of us. I should have been here. Maybe I could have saved Mama."

"Beau," his father spoke through his tears, "Beau, you always take too much on yourself. No. Perhaps it's God's mercy that you were not here. What if your mother had died while under your care?"

"I know, Daddy. But I just can't let the thought go. I loved her. Mama was so good to me. I owed it to her to be with her."

"Beau, in Philadelphia, you were exactly where God wanted you to be. You are right: your mother was, besides Jesus Christ, God's best gift to us. She loved us and she sacrificed for us. And now she is with the Lord. We'll miss her but we will see her again someday. We do not grieve as others grieve who have no hope."

Beau still clung to his father and was again awed by his humble strength and courage. What a man God had given him for a father! John Soleil was a man who walked with God.

"Beau, you need to see Grace. She has been like a daughter to us since you've been gone, like the daughter she will be when you marry her. She's tired. She's been caring for the sick since this illness broke out, going from house to house, feeding them, caring for their children, assisting Dr. Davis. Doc Davis is weary. He will be happy to see you, too."

"Daddy, I'll go and find Grace now. When will we have Mama's funeral?"

"Tomorrow morning, Beau. We had to wait to bury your mother until the ground thawed a little. It's been a little warmer the past two days. The funeral is tomorrow. Tomorrow morning at ten."

Beau left his bags just inside the door of his home and ran to find his beloved fiancée.

GRACE WAS WITH Dr. Davis as he attended to a patient just down the street. Beau knocked on the front door and was invited in by one of the children. Beau entered quietly so as not to interrupt the house call. He saw Dr. Davis listening to the lungs of his patient and just beside the sick woman was his sweetheart. Grace stood beside a washbasin and stand, towel in hand, ready to complete the woman's sponge bath. For a few seconds, they did not realize Beau had entered the room. And for those few seconds, Beau again gazed on his beloved in her natural beauty. The noon sun shining in the window behind her outlined her profile with a halo effect and it played on her brown hair, pulled up to free her for work. She was unspeakably radiant.

Grace turned her head, sensing someone else in the room, and saw Beau. She gasped, then ran crying into his arms. Her tired eyes revealed her fatigue—and her strong love. Beau clasped her to himself and they both wept tears of sadness and of joy.

"Beau, you have come. You have come!" Grace could barely speak.

Beau struggled to force his voice to utter even a whisper. He finally spoke, only faintly and quietly, "Yes, I left as soon as your letter arrived. Grace, I love you. My mother loved you. And now she's gone."

Beau continued after a few moments. "Grace, you're tired. I'm going to take care of you."

Beau turned to his old mentor. "Dr. Davis, let me take Grace home so she can get some sleep. I'll be back soon to relieve you."

"Beau, it's so good to see you. Welcome home. We need you here." Dr. Davis reached for Beau's hand to shake it and then embraced him. "I'm sorry about your mother. She was a fine woman. Yes, take Grace home and come back when you can." The weary old doctor was both relieved and overjoyed to see his young colleague.

Beau escorted Grace home, she clinging to his right arm as they walked and talked. It was good to have her near him again.

Beau ate a quick meal and soon returned to the side of Doc Davis. After having seen a few patients together, he convinced Dr. Davis to go home and sleep, and to allow Beau to handle the sick that afternoon. Beau made house calls the rest of the day, ministering to sick men and women, sick boys and girls, and offering medical care that both healed and comforted. And he also took care of far too many who that day received their last visit from a human physician.

Beau arrived back home at about 8 p.m. and ate some of the food brought over by loving church members and neighbors. Then he slept the dreamless sleep of one who is utterly spent. He awoke early the next morning and prepared for his mother's funeral.

THE SUN NEVER APPEARED that day. It was a cloudy, gray, dreary, blustery day; cold breezes were punctuated by intermittent gusts of wind like Arctic blasts. At 10 a.m., friends and fellow church members gathered in the muddy cemetery next to Sure Hope Presbyterian Church. Snowdrifts and mud made for a strange contrast. The Reverend Mr. McDonald began the service by speaking comfort from the words of Jesus himself as recorded in John's Gospel: "I am the resurrection and the life. He who believes in me, though he were dead, yet shall he live." He prayed, invoking God's presence. In the prayer, he thanked God for never leaving us or forsaking us, for the believer's future hope in Jesus that is sure and steadfast, and for the reality of the resurrection of Jesus and his followers. He thanked God for Hannah's life and the gospel lived out in it.

Mr. McDonald preached a short sermon and in it he glorified Christ, comforted family and friends, encouraged those who did not know Christ to come to him, and honored Hannah.

Just as the pastor was finishing, a sudden gust of cold wind came in from the north, blowing the gray, leafless branches of the trees. And just as suddenly, another longer blast of cold blew through the cemetery. A large, dead branch from an old oak tree overhead began to sway. It swayed back and forth in ever-increasing arcs. From below, Beau glanced at the branch, then was transfixed by it. A distant memory awakened in his mind from his previous studies in physics, something about harmonic resonance. Yes—harmonic resonance. He recognized that the wind had induced harmonic resonance in the branch. The swaying would not and could not last for long. And as the branch cracked, snapped, and broke, Beau was already moving. The branch fell like an enormous javelin to the spot of ground Doctor Davis occupied. As it fell, Beau charged Doc Davis, violently pushing him out of the way. Both men arose from the mud dirty and disheveled, but unhurt. Turning, they saw the heavy branch had speared the muck, the point buried twelve inches deep, but it had not speared them. God had spared Doc Davis. Beau could not have survived another death that day. God knew.

Reverend McDonald ended the service, gave thanks to God again, and committed Hannah to God's love. They knew her soul was in heaven and they buried her body to await the final resurrection at the return of Christ. The grayness of the day and the sadness of the occasion could not dim the bright hope of glory the congregants had in their hearts.

People greeted John and Beau, softly speaking their words of sympathy and encouragement, and slowly left for their homes. Grace stood with Beau the entire time, and she left with him, hand-in-hand, as Beau draped his left arm over John Soleil's powerful shoulder and they walked home together.

BEAU REMAINED IN Sure Hope for another two weeks. He helped his father arrange his affairs and he assisted Dr. Davis in patient care. The spread of illness slowed and finally ceased. Twenty-nine people perished that winter in Sure Hope.

Beau and Grace spent every bit of free time together. After a few days, Beau had a sudden burst of inspiration and insight.

"Grace, we should get married." He spoke slowly and deliberately, as a man should when discussing a serious topic.

"But Beau, we *are* getting married. In June. Remember?" Grace didn't understand.

"No, Grace, I mean *now*. Now. We should get married now. This week. Then you can come with me to Philadelphia for a few months, and we'll come back here to start our new life together. I don't want to wait until June. I need you with me in Philadelphia." Beau was not being impulsive or impetuous. He simply saw things as they were and made a bold decision.

"Beau, yes! Yes!! I'll talk with my parents. No, let's both talk with my parents now. I think they will agree and I think we can arrange the wedding quickly."

They spoke with Grace's parents, Joshua and Miriam McLeod, who after a few moments of surprise, realized that there was really no reason to wait and consented to the earlier wedding. They loved Beau and knew he was the man for Grace. They could not arrange for the wedding to happen for another ten days, but arrange it they did.

Thus, on February 27, 1889, Beau and Grace Soleil became husband and wife. It was a small, simple ceremony presided over by Reverend McDonald and attended by close family and friends. John Soleil was best man, and Grace's only sister, Martha, was maid of honor. Of course, Wes Threlkeld and his family were there, along with Dr. and Mrs. Davis, the Argentas, and a few others.

The young couple spent the next few days and nights at the home of Mr. and Mrs. Argenta; the Argentas had graciously offered for Beau and Grace to honeymoon in the Argenta mansion. On the second floor, a bridal suite awaited the newlyweds, prepared with love by the Argentas. The Argentas escorted Beau and Grace upstairs to their room where a fire roared in the fireplace and the bed was bedecked with dried rose petals. Beau and Grace spent the next three days in and around the Argenta home where Mr. and Mrs. Argenta saw to their every need. They were exhausted and needed rest. For three days, Beau and Grace went for refreshing sleigh rides in the freshly fallen snow and they took long, intimate walks in the silent woods. They read and they thought. They visited with the Argentas and with a few friends and family. And they often retreated to their bridal chamber for long conversations.

SOON AFTERWARDS, Beau and Grace traveled to Philadelphia and converted Beau's former bachelor room to that of a married couple. Mrs. Harrison was delighted to have Grace in her home and treated her like a daughter. Beau was delighted to have his young bride with him. And Grace was delighted to be able to experience Beau's life with him in Philadelphia.

Beau saw, treated, and learned from hundreds of patients over the next months. A memorable encounter occurred in late March. He was called to the emergency area to care for a man with a hand laceration.

Upon entering the exam room, Beau saw a black man in his fifties. He was seated and seemed to be in mild pain but no distress. He appeared to be prosperous, dressed as he was in a black suit, white shirt, tie, and vest. A gold watch chain and fob were attached to his pocket watch tucked away in his vest. His black bowler hat had been carefully placed on a table. The man cradled his left hand in his right. His left hand was wrapped in a tightly wound, bloody bandage.

"Good afternoon," Beau greeted the man with a smile as he walked in and observed the situation. "I'm Beau Soleil. I'll be taking care of you today. It looks like you hurt your hand."

"Hello, Dr. Soleil. I'm George Smith." He returned Beau's smile. "Thank you for seeing me. I would shake your hand but, as you can see, it is a little inconvenient for me now. Yes, I cut my hand an hour ago. I was slicing an apple in my hand and the knife slipped. My eyesight is not what it used to be and I think I was in a hurry. The knife was sharp. A sharp knife, poor eyesight, a slippery apple, and a man in a rush are a dangerous combination." George Smith's eyes twinkled as he wryly described the accident, both embarrassed and amused by how it all had occurred.

"I'm sorry to hear you cut yourself. Well, Mr. Smith, let's take a look." And Beau gently and deftly unwrapped the bandage to examine his hand. He had a clean, fairly superficial laceration across the entire palm of his left hand. To prevent bleeding, Beau held his hand up and intermittently compressed the hand with a new bandage as he examined it. He made certain that no tendons were cut. And then he spoke again.

"Mr. Smith, I'll need to put a few stitches in your hand but it should heal quickly and well. Do you mind if I proceed?"

"Please fix it, Doctor. But first… if you don't mind, may I ask you… I hesitate to ask… have you ever done anything like this before? You seem mighty young."

"I'm young, Mr. Smith, but yes, I've done many repairs like this. And I have had excellent training. I think you'll like the outcome."

With George Smith's consent, Beau set about cleansing and then repairing the laceration.

As is common, the doctor and his patient carried on a conversation during the repair.

"Dr. Soleil, you don't seem to be from around here. You don't talk like you're from Philadelphia. My ear tells me you're from down south."

"You have a good ear, sir. I'm from Virginia." Beau always enjoyed these conversations.

"What town are you from?"

"I come from a little town in western Virginia called Sure Hope."

"Sure Hope. Interesting. I've been near there before."

"Really, Mr. Smith? That's unusual. Very few people have ever even heard of it. I love it there and plan to return. But hardly anybody knows it exists. Why were you there?"

"Doctor, I was born a slave. I found my way to freedom

through the Underground Railroad. My route passed through a station near Sure Hope many years ago."

Beau pondered these words for a few minutes as he sutured the wound, then voiced his thoughts. "I have heard rumors that there was an Underground Railroad station near Sure Hope. Slavery was a hideous thing. I've never understood how humans could justify owning other humans. Slavery creates the situation where the slave is viewed and treated as less than human. Slavery injures and deforms the soul of the owner. Thank God it is illegal and abolished now; it was always immoral. You must have endured suffering beyond anything I can imagine. I sympathize with you. I admire your courage and strength."

Beau continued his thoughts as he sewed and then spoke again, musing aloud. "Hmm—a few years ago, I read a book by William Still called *The Underground Railroad Records*. I understand Mr. Still lives in Philadelphia. Do you know him?"

"Know him, Doctor? Know him? Yes! He is a good friend. I've worked with him for years. After I found my way north, I ended up in Philadelphia. William Still is a fine man. Only God knows how many slaves found freedom and help through him."

"I'd like to meet him. I have met his daughter. You may know Dr. Caroline Anderson?"

"Yes, I know her. She's out of town now. She is my doctor."

"Well, you have a fine physician. I'm glad I could repair your hand in her absence. We've just about finished. Your hand will heal well. I'll wrap it in a bandage. I'm going to put you in a sling for a few days. Keep your hand clean and dry. Keep it elevated and rest it on a pillow tonight as your sleep. I recommend you see Dr. Anderson in about two or three days for a recheck. She'll likely remove the sutures in about seven days. And Mr. Smith, it has been a pleasure meeting you and talking with you."

"Thank you, Dr. Soleil. You have taken good care of me. I wish you well."

The men rose from their seats. Each man recognized that he had just encountered a kindred spirit. Beau respected George Smith's quiet dignity and confidence. George Smith appreciated the big, young physician's honest humility and gentleness.

They shook hands and looked each other in the eye. They resolved to spend time together, and over the next few months, they would manage a few short visits. They would become friends, and their friendship would make a mark on both men.

And after George Smith left that day, Beau Soleil treasured their conversation in his heart, turning it over and over. He never did meet William Still. But he intended to investigate where in the Sure Hope area the Underground Railroad station had been.

THE FEW MONTHS REMAINING in Philadelphia sped by. Spring came early and the city was resplendent with prophetic pale-green leaves sprouting from stately trees, and with majestic flowers blooming from humble plants. The sun shone, and the Soleils thought back to their home in Sure Hope, Virginia. It would not be long before their time in Philadelphia was over and they would be home for good. But for now, they would enjoy God's creation and the city of Philadelphia.

They celebrated Easter on April 21st at West Spruce Street Presbyterian Church. It was glorious for Beau and Grace to worship with hundreds of other believers and hear the pastor proclaim, "Christ is risen!" With hearts full of joy, they joined in the antiphonal response with other worshipers: "He is risen indeed. Alleluia!" They sang the hymns celebrating the resurrection. Dr. William Pratt Breed preached on John 20, the beautiful, miraculous, history-altering account of the saving resurrection of Jesus Christ from the dead.

With gladness and gratitude, Beau and Grace accepted an invitation for lunch from the Hoffmans, an elderly couple at the church. They had met just that day. The Hoffmans had noticed Beau and Grace as visitors to their church. During the worship service, Mrs. Hoffman kept looking at Beau as if she knew him. She could not place him and she remained puzzled; she wondered if she

was confusing him with someone else. The Hoffmans asked
for Beau and Grace to join them and their extended family
at their home. They enveloped them into their family and
lavished love and grace on the newlyweds. With thanks,
they all enjoyed the feast spread before them.

During the meal, Beau and Grace told the family a
little about themselves. Mrs. Hoffman, usually animated
and talkative, was unusually quiet as she studied Beau and
searched her memory. Who *was* he?

Beau discussed his medical work as Mrs. Hoffman
listened to the voice and the stories, eyes half-closed, and
pondered the mystery. Who *was* this young man? And
suddenly, with a start and a smile, Mrs. Hoffman knew
him. His voice sealed her recognition.

"Beau," Mrs. Hoffman began, "I have a story for you. I
think you may find it interesting."

"Please proceed, Mrs. Hoffman. I love a good story."
Beau settled back in his chair and listened carefully.

"A few months ago, in early February, I became ill. It
was during the epidemic. I was so sick that I was admitted
to the hospital. I developed pneumonia. I became deathly
sick. I almost died." She paused for a moment.

"Please go on." Beau could not discern the point of the
story yet but he was glad she had survived.

"Early one morning, soon after I was admitted, I
suddenly made a turn for the worse. I could not breathe. I

thought I was dying. I was frightened. I became confused and agitated. I can't remember much more about it, but they tell me that a kind young physician rushed to the hospital and saved my life."

Beau interjected here, "Mrs. Hoffman, what did he do? How did he save your life?" He hoped to learn something from her story that might help his future patients.

"They tell me he placed a needle in the back of my chest and drew off pus and fluid. The procedure, they tell me, is called a thoracentesis. I don't remember it. I have a hazy impression of a kind man speaking gently to me but that's all I can remember. I never saw the doctor again after that day. They told me he had a family emergency and had to leave the city. I never saw him again. I left the hospital a few days later to go home to recover. And now, I'm back to normal."

Beau listened with his eyes firmly fixed on Mrs. Hoffman's face, now with tears staining her cheeks. He began to see.

"Beau, I have a question for you. Where were you early on the morning of February 9?" Mrs. Hoffman put the question which by this time needed no answer. She gave Beau time to think about it.

Mrs. Hoffman, now softly weeping, ended the story. "Beau, that doctor was you. God used you to save my life."

The memory came flooding back to Beau and he

remembered everything. In vain, he attempted to hide his tears and emotion as he realized that here was the woman whose life he had rescued just three days after his own mother had died—of the same disease and complications.

Beau explained to the entire group why he had left Philadelphia so suddenly after he had treated Mrs. Hoffman. They all expressed their sorrow at his mother's premature death.

After a few minutes of silent reflection, during which everyone tried to take in and process the events just discussed, and to wonder at the kind Providence of God, Mrs. Hoffman went on. "Beau, I know now why I didn't recognize you before now. That day, I was confused and incoherent. That is true. But there is something else. I have one more question for you. How long have you worn a beard?"

Beau smiled now. "I grew a beard soon after we married. Grace likes it. I did it for her."

"I would have recognized you if not for the beard. I never forget a face. Or a voice." Mrs. Hoffman was firm in her conviction. And looking into Beau's eyes she said, "Thank you, Dr. Soleil. Thank you."

Easter dinner at the Hoffmans was full of joy, gratitude, and unexpected revelation. The Hoffmans and the Soleils became fast friends that day and remained so for the rest of their lives.

AND AS BEAU AND GRACE ambled home together that afternoon, hand holding hand, exulting in God's goodness and mercy, in their resurrected Savior, in the beauty and aroma of springtime, and in each other, they were overcome with joy.

Beau stopped his slow walk, slipped his arm around Grace's waist, and gently turned her to himself. He peered into her deep, unfathomable eyes and gazed into her guileless face. Beau pulled her close and kissed her.

And he whispered into his bride's ear, "Grace, I love you."

JUST BEFORE THE SOLEILS left Philadelphia, Beau came home with a surprise. As a way of showing his appreciation to Beau for all his hard work, his attending physician, Dr. Parker, had given Beau two tickets to a concert by The Philharmonic Society of New York who were on a grand tour of the great eastern cities.

"Grace, I have a little present for you," Beau said as he hugged and kissed his bride. He knew Grace loved surprises and she loved good music.

"What is it, Beau?"

"It's a surprise. I can't tell you now." Beau was playing with Grace.

"Please, Beau. Tell me what it is!"

"No, it's a surprise. It's a secret. I think surprises are

always secret. I can't tell you what it is. If I told you now, it wouldn't be a surprise, would it?" He smiled.

"Beau, I know you're just teasing me. Come on, Beau. What is it?"

"Alright, Grace. If you insist. Look inside this envelope." He pulled a white envelope out of his pocket and handed it to her. He anticipated her girlish delight when she saw the contents. He loved to make his wife happy.

Grace tore open the envelope and withdrew the tickets. "Oh, Beau! This is wonderful! How did you get these? These tickets cost a lot. Did they really cost you $2 each? Can we afford it?"

"Don't worry, Gracie. Dr. Parker gave them to me. This is his parting gift to you and me."

The concert occurred the next night, June 15. Grace and Beau wore their best and most formal clothes. As Grace emerged from their bedroom, Beau was overcome by her beauty. She was stunning in her black velvet gown. A black ribbon was in her long hair. Around her fair neck, she wore a strand of white pearls, a wedding gift from her mother. Grace smiled at Beau. He could not help kissing her.

"Grace, you are beautiful," he spoke tenderly to her as he thought to himself, "Thank God for a pretty wife!"

A carriage arrived for them at 7 p.m. and dropped

them off at the concert hall. Their seats were on row five in the center section. Beau was grateful that his seat was on the aisle which allowed ample room for his long legs.

They took in the atmosphere as the musicians tuned their instruments. The aristocrats of Philadelphia were all there. The Soleils felt out of place but they enjoyed the almost palpable excitement and vitality.

Beau's mind wandered back to his boyhood days when he had experienced his first serious concert—the one when Melody Grimm Manypenny serenaded the citizens of Sure Hope. He hoped this concert would be a little better. He did not expect to hear dogs howling or sheriffs bursting in to make arrests.

The maestro entered and the concert began. The orchestra performed Beethoven's Symphony No. 9 in D Minor, Opus 125. The audience listened to the glorious piece as it proceeded to the choral section and reached its climax with Ode to Joy. The music profoundly moved everyone.

Few things in the universe have more power than beauty. Beauty has power to melt the cold heart and power to break the hard heart. Beauty can make the tender heart weep. Beauty can make a person look to God and say, "Thank you!"

When the orchestra played its last note, the crowd spontaneously rose to their feet in standing ovation. They had been touched by joy and beauty. Beau and Grace knew they had just experienced something they might not ever know again.

The Soleils left the concert hall with smiles on their faces and in their hearts. God had blessed them yet again. They looked forward to the future where God would be there also, leading them and blessing them, crowning their lives with his steadfast love and faithfulness.

And they prepared to return to Sure Hope in a few short days.

13

COMING HOME

BEAU AND GRACE SOLEIL left Philadelphia and returned home to Sure Hope on July 2, 1889. They traveled by train to Winchester, transporting all their belongings in a few carpetbags. They arrived in Sure Hope by stagecoach in the early afternoon. The open windows allowed the cool mountain air and the delicious aroma of sweet mountain grass to fill the passenger compartment. They breathed deeply of the welcoming atmosphere. They smiled at each other. They were home.

John Soleil and Grace's parents, Joshua and Miriam McLeod, were there to greet them. Wolf was also part of the reception party; he had stayed behind with John during the months Beau had been in Philadelphia. Wolf was now nervously running around waiting for his master. He knew he was coming home.

Beau opened the door of the stagecoach and leapt out before the wheels stopped rolling. He ran toward John and hugged him but not before Wolf almost knocked them both down in his rambunctious joy. Beau and John kissed each other. Beau never felt embarrassed to kiss his father. It was good to feel the embrace of his strong father again. "Daddy, it's good to be home again!" Beau exclaimed.

He turned to help Grace down the steps of the stagecoach and she ran into the arms of her father and mother, all with tears of joy in their eyes. Grace hugged and kissed John.

In the background was Mr. James Argenta. He was getting old now. He smiled and felt satisfaction in knowing that this fine young doctor was back in Sure Hope; he was grateful that he had been able to play a role in making this event happen. He ambled toward Beau, extended his hand to shake Beau's, and warmly said, "Welcome home, Dr. Soleil. It's good to have you back!"

Sure Hope was decorated for Independence Day. American flags adorned buildings. Red, white, and blue bunting hung from railings and red, white, and blue banners streamed from poles. The wounds of 1865 were healing and people were glad to be one nation. They were proud and grateful to be citizens of the United States of America. Children were especially excited about the holiday because they knew what lay ahead. July 4th would be a day of fun and feasting.

BEAU AND GRACE LIVED with her parents for a few days. They had arranged to rent a small home in town. It had four rooms: two bedrooms, a living room, and a kitchen. Beau would use the spare bedroom as a study for now. They would move in after July 4th. There was still a little to be done to prepare the home. Furniture and furnishings were generously provided by their parents and a few friends. Some of the pieces of furniture from others appeared to be cast-offs, because they were. Beau would need to repair some of it. But the home would be theirs.

The young couple went to bed early that evening. They were exhausted but thrilled to be back home with family and friends—back home in the mountains—back home in Sure Hope.

THEY HAD A FEW visitors during their first days at the McLeods' house. Some good friends, including Wes Threlkeld and his wife, dropped by to wish them well. Beau's old schoolteachers congratulated him on having finished his training. Mrs. Huffnagle, his favorite teacher, came by to say hello and to tell him how proud she was of him. And the new mayor, Mr. William Arcangelo Seraphicus Pride, and his wife Serena made an official visit to welcome the new doctor. Mr. Pride had arrived in Sure Hope during Beau's eight years away and somehow had wormed his way into the community to finally land the job of mayor. Mr.

Pride loved all these official "state visits" as he called them. He loved to demonstrate to the town and to the world his great importance. He was a peacock who dressed in all the finery and foppery of the day. He thought he was a gamecock and in his mind he was king of the aviary. In reality, he was a bantam rooster who did not need to walk in order to strut.

Mr. Pride talked in a studied, affected way: slowly, deeply, and importantly. He had an impressive bookshelf full of impressive books; he had even read one or two of them (the one or two that had lots of illustrations). He was arrogant, pompous, and full of self.

He was generally insufferable.

Mrs. Serena Pride was a nervous woman, given to fits of emotional outbursts, crying easily, worrying endlessly, and anxious constantly; somehow her name did not fit her. She talked far too much, especially when she was nervous. One could say she never stopped talking, except when she was sick or asleep. But she was a good-hearted woman.

Mr. William Arcangelo Seraphicus Pride strode into the home, and with a flourish, doffed his hat and bowed, saying, "Welcome to my city, Dr. Soleil. If I may ever be of any help to you, please let me know. I hope you are able to help our people, though, as I am sure you know, my wife and I, and those of us who can afford to, all go to Charlottesville or Richmond for the best medical care."

Beau Soleil took a deep breath, restrained himself from saying what he was thinking, and thanked the mayor. Beau hardly knew Mr. Pride. But he did know this: he knew he did not like him. It was not really hatred. How can you hate someone you don't know? He just did not like him—at all. It was all instinct. He also knew he actually felt some secret pleasure in not liking him. He felt guilty about this but could not help himself. He hoped they would leave soon. He also hoped he would not have to shake Mr. Pride's hand.

Mr. Pride stayed longer than he should have, but he needed to impress upon everyone his importance. Finally, he took his leave. Sure enough, Mr. Pride stuck out his hand for a friendly departing handshake and Beau gave him the obligatory shake. Mr. Pride's hand felt like a dead, cold, limp, greasy fish; his hand was oily with hair pomade or cologne or something else. Maybe he was just an oily person. Mr. Pride would not let go, kept shaking, and moved closer to Beau's face as he said, "Beau, call on me if you need me." Beau was treated to his malodorous breath, a delicate combination of cigars, onions, and poor dental hygiene. Beau thanked Mr. Pride despite his dislike for him. When Mr. Pride finally released Beau's hand, Beau could not help reflexively glancing at his hand for any residue. Nothing visible being there, he still wiped his hand on his trouser leg. The Prides eventually left, much to Beau's relief.

THE FOURTH OF JULY arrived and it seemed the entire community came to town. People took at least part of the day off to celebrate. Children arose early, some of them before the sun came up, with eager anticipation.

At about ten o'clock, the festivities began. Mr. Pride felt it his duty as mayor (it was part of his official mayoral responsibility—besides, he liked being in front of a crowd) to welcome everyone, and he offered up the usual trite, boring, and self-serving speech that lasted too long. The crowd politely listened—and endured. When he came to the end, or near the end (it was hard to tell), when he finally stopped to pause, the crowd gave a great cheer. The cheer was not for the sparkling speech or for the arrogant mayor: they cheered because the speech was finally over.

The local band played patriotic music. Lemonade in cool pitchers flowed like mountain streams. Slices of watermelon made their way into sticky hands of children and by noon, watermelon juice covered the clothes of many of Sure Hope's finest. Far too many watermelon seeds became missiles launched from the mouths of mischievous boys. The boys were great believers in equality: after all, they were Americans. To their everlasting credit, the boys were absolutely egalitarian in that they spat the seeds on anyone near enough to hit; it did not matter whether the targets were men or women, boys or girls, tall or short, wealthy or poor. Any target would do. They found that sitting in second floor windows offered strategic vantage points and launch platforms. Those who choose the high ground usually win.

At twelve o'clock, everyone gathered as family units for a picnic lunch. Under the shade of a mighty oak, the McLeods and Soleils devoured fried chicken, potato salad, deviled eggs, sliced tomatoes and cucumbers, and pickles. Families feasted. Good will abounded. And citizens of the best country ever established thanked God, celebrated, and reveled in their freedom.

After lunch, the two big events of the day were the pie contest and children's games. The pie contest was first. The greatest cooks in the area baked their pies and then competed for bragging rights. Beau Soleil, as the returning son of Sure Hope and the town's new physician, was granted the high privilege of judging the pie contest. He did not hesitate to accept the honor. His co-adjudicator was Mr. Argenta.

As families were finishing lunch, Beau and Mr. Argenta made their way to several makeshift tables groaning with the weight of beautiful pies. They tasted thirty-one pies that afternoon. There were pecan, apple, blueberry, and blackberry pies; there were peach cobblers. All were deemed superlative. However, the job of the judges was to choose three finalists. They narrowed the finalists to a pecan pie, a blackberry pie, and an apple pie.

They rang a bell and the crowd gathered around the pies. With much ceremony, the judges carefully re-tasted the last three pies and commented on each one's flavor, texture, appearance, and aroma. After they withdrew for a few minutes to consult in private, Beau and Mr. Argenta re-emerged and announced the winner. They gave the gold medal to Mrs. Hephzibah Whetstone whose blackberry pie, they proclaimed, was heavenly. The crowd erupted with a huge round of applause as Mrs. Whetstone proudly accepted the award and slipped the gold medal around her neck.

GAMES WERE NEXT ON the agenda. Excited children ran to the games area, a shady grass-covered clearing near the river. Adults watched in sleepy, satisfied post-prandial trances as children squealed and shouted and laughed. The children loved the games. They played pin-the-tail-on-the-donkey. They bobbed for apples. They had races of every kind. They had sprints. They had three-legged, sack, relay, and wheel-barrow races. Afterwards, the children went into the river to wade and swim to cool down. They ended with a larded watermelon relay race in the river.

It was fun for Beau to see some children of his boyhood friends and acquaintances. Wes Threlkeld's son, Luke, was six years old. Rufus Crabtree had a son also, Rufus, Jr. who was called Junior. They both reminded Beau of their fathers.

AFTER THE GAMES, everyone gathered for dessert at the pie tables. As they did, they heard a loud shriek. It came from Mrs. Beulah Abernathy, whose apple pie had claimed second place in the pie contest. She was screaming and crying. Her pie was missing. "Someone stole my pie! Someone stole my pie!!" Her husband, Jacob, came to her aid and tried to comfort her. He whispered to her, "Beulah, calm down. Calm down."

That was exactly what Beulah did not want to hear. "Jake, don't tell me to calm down! Someone stole my pie!!" She raised the volume and shrieked more loudly, "Someone stole my pie!!" She would not be consoled.

AROUND THE CORNER LAY a sick boy. He was lying on his side and whimpering. He was pale—no, he was a shade of light green.

That morning he had been boisterous and full of enthusiasm. After all, it was July Fourth. He was an American boy. He should celebrate. He did. Maybe a little too much. He had consumed three slices of watermelon. He had downed at least six glasses of lemonade. And at lunch he had feasted like it was his last meal on earth. Afterwards, he had run and raced and jumped as hard as all the other children.

During the games, he felt his stomach sloshing a little. He was a little queasy. But he remembered that there was pie for dessert. Before the others could notice, he left the games early and stealthily made his way to the pie tables. No one was there. What was a boy to do? In front of him was an irresistible temptation: an untended apple pie. Who could blame him if he yielded? He could not help himself. He took the apple pie and ran behind a building. Then he ate the whole thing—the whole thing.

Rufus Crabtree looked for his son, Junior, after the games and couldn't find him. Junior was missing. He asked friends and family but no one had seen him. He finally found him lying on his side, moaning and groaning, whimpering and whining. There was an empty pie pan beside him. It was completely apparent what had happened.

"Hi, Daddy. I feel so sick," Junior murmured.

"Yes, you look pretty sick, Junior. Did you eat the whole pie? I mean, by yourself?" Before Rufus Crabtree, Sr. could finish his interrogation, he was interrupted by Junior.

"Daddy, I feel sick. I think I'm going to throw up." Junior was moaning again. Then Junior threw up. He vomited everything. And then he felt better. He turned to his father with a smile. "Hi, Daddy. I feel fine now."

His father cleaned him up the best he could but Junior reeked of stomach contents.

They went back to the pie tables to try to make amends. Rufus Crabtree, Sr. had grown up to become a respectable citizen and a good father. They found Mrs.

Abernathy. Junior confessed to his crime and begged her forgiveness—on his knees. It was a truly dramatic confession. If there had been an award for acting that day, he would have won. Mrs. Beulah Abernathy had calmed down by then and told Junior she forgave him. The awful odor on his clothes and breath told her that the little miscreant had suffered enough for his sin.

And so, it became evident that seven-year-old Rufus Crabtree, Jr. was a pie-lover, just like his daddy. The Crabtree males had a hereditary weakness for apple pie. It was clear that Junior could not help himself when an apple pie was nearby. The temptation was too great.

The apple never falls far from the tree. Nor does the crabapple from the Crabtree.

WHEN BEAU AND HIS BRIDE returned to Sure Hope, there was one thing they revealed to their parents but to no one else, at least not then: Grace was three months pregnant. The family was excited. No—they were ecstatic.

Life was busy for the young Soleils. They enjoyed their little house and Grace transformed it into a home. Beau's medical practice was almost non-stop. Grace provided a refuge of rest for a weary and burdened doctor.

Grace's pregnancy proceeded normally and without any problems. By December, she was ready to deliver. She was tired, she was not sleeping well, and her legs were swollen.

On December 24, 1889, Grace Soleil went into labor. At 2 a.m. on December 25, Grace gave birth to a daughter, delivered by her father, Dr. Beau Soleil. (Dr. Davis had stopped delivering babies several years before.) The little girl was fair-skinned and her hair was reddish-brown; she looked like her mother. Grace was exhausted from labor and slept well the rest of the night. Beau, as all fathers are, was frightened during Grace's labor that something might happen to his wife and baby. Mothers bear awful physical suffering during labor. Fathers endure horrible psychological anguish and fear. An added fear was this: Beau was also afraid that his skills would somehow fail him as he delivered his own baby. Beau prayed all night for them all. He was relieved at the safe arrival of his baby. After the delivery, he slept fitfully in a chair as he kept watch over his little family.

They named their daughter Christina Grace. She was their Christmas baby. And Grace and Beau thanked God with all their hearts.

Sure Hope celebrated Christmas and word traveled quickly that the Soleils had a new baby girl. The Soleils celebrated the birth of their Savior and the birthdays of Beau and Christina. It was a triple celebration.

Christina would grow into a girl who was just like her mother in looks and demeanor and makeup. She was a born leader. She burned with fiery passion and intensity. She loved people deeply and she hated injustice just as deeply. She would become a beloved big sister to her siblings.

EIGHTEEN MONTHS LATER, another Soleil child arrived safely, a son. There was a little difficulty in the delivery because he was a large baby and had broad shoulders. He was much like his father had been as a baby. He was a big-chested, broad-shouldered boy with a big head covered in dark brown hair. Beau noticed that there seemed to be pain when the boy moved his left arm. Feeling the shoulder and arm, Beau felt some crepitance (squishiness) and slight swelling over the mid-shaft of the collar bone. The baby was tender there. He had a clavicle fracture. Beau knew the fracture would heal without treatment. He warned everyone who handled the baby to avoid much movement of the left arm and to not put pressure on the left collar bone. He also let Grace know that within a few weeks there would be a hard swelling over the area. "Don't worry, Grace, he will be fine. The bone will heal and there will be no problem." One of a doctor's favorite sayings to his family members is "he will be fine" or "you will be fine." Beau was right. The bone healed just fine.

The boy was calm and serious. He nursed well, but even when he was hungry he cried little. He spent much of his waking time peering and gazing silently and seriously at the loving faces and the interesting objects surrounding him. It was not easy to know what deep thoughts this baby had at this age, nor would it be easy to penetrate his mind as he grew older.

His name was John Peter Soleil. They called him Johnny. His blacksmith grandfather had a namesake, and John Soleil began to plan all he would teach young Johnny Soleil.

THE SOLEILS WELCOMED ANOTHER baby into their world of love and grace two years after Johnny was born. His birthday was May 30, 1893. This baby boy was named Joshua Andrew Soleil, in honor of Grace's father. The delivery was Grace's easiest yet. This boy looked and acted much like Johnny; they could have been twins separated by two years. Little Joshua was the perfect baby. He fed well and cried little. By this time, the Soleils were relaxed with their babies. They enjoyed Joshua without worrying too much about him. Grace delighted in caring for her new infant son. She enjoyed nursing him, holding him, rocking him, and singing to him. Grace was full of happiness and joy. Christina was old enough, at age three and a half, to help her mother. She delighted in cradling Joshua in her arms and talking and singing to him. She was a little mother. Grace's mother, Miriam McLeod, spent a week at the Soleil home caring for the family as Grace recovered.

The little home was getting small for their needs, and

Beau began to think of their next home for his quickly growing family. For now, Christina and Johnny slept in one bedroom and Joshua was in his crib in his parents' bedroom.

When Joshua was eleven days old, Beau went to his crib to see if his newest son was ready to feed. It was about 6 a.m. and the sun was just shining its early light through the window. Beau crept quietly to the crib so as not to awaken the sleeping baby or anyone else in the small house. He gazed with love at his son but noticed something strange. Joshua was not moving and he was not breathing. His color was a bluish gray. Beau reached for his son and quickly picked him up in his arms, holding him over his shoulder. Joshua had no muscle tone; he was floppy. His skin was cold. Beau firmly patted his back, gently at first, then harder, to stimulate him. He could not arouse him. Beau tried to hold back his fears and his tears but could not. He called for Grace as he simultaneously laid Joshua on their bed. "Grace, wake up. Something's wrong with Joshua!"

Grace quickly slid out of bed and rushed to Beau's side. She knew immediately. Their baby was not moving or breathing. Beau had tears in his eyes and tears on his cheeks and a look of terror on his face. Beau placed his ear to Joshua's heart. There was nothing. Beau attempted mouth to mouth resuscitation by placing his mouth over Joshua's nose and mouth and exhaling to expand Joshua's lungs. He repeated this procedure over the course of several minutes. His efforts were futile. Joshua never started to breathe and his heart rate never returned.

The meaning could not be clearer. Their beautiful son was dead. He had died sometime during the wee hours of the morning.

A thought briefly flashed into Beau's mind: "Physician, heal thyself." And sorrow and guilt and grief overwhelmed him like a flood.

BEAU AND GRACE TOGETHER picked up their beloved son and together sat on their bed as they cradled him and wept. They sobbed as they held Joshua and clung to each other. Simultaneously, the verse from the weeping prophet Jeremiah came to their minds: *A voice is heard in Ramah, lamentation and bitter weeping, Rachel is weeping for her children, she refuses to be comforted for her children, because they are no more.*

Joshua was no more on this earth.

BEAU AND GRACE STAYED in their room a long time. Through tears, they prayed. They asked God why. "Why, God?" God is near the brokenhearted. God knows when we hurt and when we cannot produce much more of a prayer than, "God, help me." Or, "Christ, have mercy on me." God does not expect us to go through life unfeeling, not grieving at the sickness and death and fallenness we all experience. He may not answer our questions now, but he is near us and with us, loving and caring for us. They thanked God for this baby who had given them such joy for a short time. They thanked God for each other and for Christina and Johnny. And they thanked God for his Son, Jesus Christ, and the hope of the resurrection. They knew they did not grieve as others grieve who do not know the Lord and have no hope. They knew their son was alive in heaven with Jesus Christ. They knew they would see Joshua again. They knew God would tenderly be with them and tend their broken hearts with comfort and nearness.

They trusted God's goodness.

BEAU EMERGED FROM THEIR room and first talked with his mother-in-law, Miriam McLeod. She was busy getting breakfast ready for the family. "Miriam, I have something to tell you. Please step outside for a moment."

Miriam sensed that something awful was coming. She looked at Beau's reddened eyes and grave expression. She followed him through the front door.

Beau turned to her and tried to explain while controlling his emotions. "Miriam, Joshua has just died. I found him an hour ago in the crib. He was lifeless. I tried to revive him. He is gone. I don't know why. But he is gone."

Miriam emitted an involuntary wail. "No!! This can't

be! He was fine when I held him last night." She wept and could not be consoled. Beau drew her to himself and tried to comfort her. She realized that she needed to cry softly so as not to frighten the children. She was crushed but steadied herself to go back into the house to care for little Christina and Johnny. First she went to Grace and hugged her neck. Together, they trembled and wept bitter tears of grief. Then, Miriam dried her eyes, composed herself, and finished preparing breakfast for the children.

Beau, in the meantime, had gathered the children to himself in a large chair. Christina was the first to speak.

"Daddy, what's wrong? Daddy, why are you crying?"

"Christina and Johnny, I want to tell you something. Last night, Joshua was happy and healthy. This morning when I checked on him, he had left us and gone to heaven. He is in heaven now with Jesus."

Both Christina and Johnny buried their heads in their father's bosom and cried. He wrapped his arms around them and held them close as he silently wept. The children could not understand death (who does?) but they knew that their little brother was no longer with them. They knew the adults in the house were all crying. They knew that a deep wound had been inflicted on their family. They cried with broken hearts as little children who must face death very early in life.

THE SHOCKING NEWS OF Joshua's death spread through Sure Hope and all over town people began praying. This type of thing was not supposed to happen to a child, and especially to a doctor's child. But it did, and it does. Pastor McDonald came to the house as soon as he heard and he arrived at the same time as John Soleil. Together they entered the home and hugged the family. Then they sat down with them and mourned with them and prayed with them.

Friends and acquaintances began coming to the house, not staying long, but offering the Soleils their sympathy. They brought food for the family. They attempted to show their love and attempted to share the burden.

ON JUNE 13, 1893, Joshua Andrew Soleil was buried after a heart-lacerating worship service at the graveside. Reverend McDonald led the service and began with the text, *Precious in the sight of the Lord is the death of his saints.* The large gathering sang the Doxology together: "Praise God from whom all blessings flow..." They said the Lord's Prayer together. And Pastor McDonald labored hard to do what Beau and Grace Soleil had requested. He sought to honor the Lord, to comfort family and friends, to honor the short life of Joshua Andrew, and to make clear the gospel of Jesus Christ. With many tears, little Joshua was lowered into the grave. With much hope, Beau and Grace knew he was present in heaven with Jesus Christ and that his body would be resurrected at the last day. They would see him again.

BEAU AND GRACE NEVER got over the death of Joshua. The death of a child is not something anyone ever gets over. God does not expect us to. The death of a child is not something we expect. It is not natural. It is a deep gash that only God can heal, if not in time, then in eternity.

Privately, they took time every May 30th to remember his birthday and grieve their loss. Every May 30th they placed a little baby rattle on Grace's dresser; it had been artfully crafted for Joshua before his birth by his blacksmith grandfather. God seemed especially near them on those days. And they kept moving on in life, caring for and loving the living. They had children, parents, and friends who needed them, and whom they needed.

IN SEPTEMBER 1894, Grace again became pregnant. And on June 15, 1895, a new baby arrived safely in the Soleil household. Her name was Miriam Hannah in honor of her grandmothers. And a beautiful little girl she was. She had dark hair. She was petite. She was a happy child who smiled from the time she was born. She had dimples on both cheeks. She looked like Miriam McLeod, her maternal grandmother.

Little Miriam brought much joy to the Soleils and to everyone who knew her. Grace again was singing with delight as she nursed and cared for her. To Christina, Miriam was a personal baby doll. To Johnny, Miriam was a little sister who needed his tender protection. And to Beau, Miriam was salve for a wounded heart. A joyful heart is good medicine.

SIX YEARS AFTER HIS return to Sure Hope, Beau Soleil had a busy practice and a full family. July 4th rolled around again the summer of 1895. Sure Hope celebrated as usual. The Soleils participated with all their hearts and they participated with hearts full of joy. Christina and Johnny were old enough to take part in the games. Luke Threlkeld and Junior Crabtree took care of them like they were their big brothers. Grace carried little Miriam around in her arms, keeping her in the shade and making sure she did not get too hot.

And Dr. Beau Soleil again judged the pie contest. He was rapidly becoming the permanent pie judge, the resident pie expert, an occupation he did not mind too much.

And this year, there were no sick little boys with empty pie pans beside them.

14

TERROR AT MIDNIGHT

BEAU SOLEIL OPENED HIS office for patients on July 22,1889. There is an important story from this period in his history that needs to be told. It occurred soon after his return to Sure Hope.

By the time he began his practice, Beau Soleil had spent more than two weeks preparing the office with needed equipment, supplies, and organization. It surprised him to see the many patients who came in that first day. Most of them were poor. Most of the ailments and illnesses were minor, though some were complex. Beau enjoyed the satisfaction that he was well prepared to practice medicine. The day went surprisingly smoothly. Beau enjoyed his new practice and both he and it flourished.

Because many of his patients could not come to his office, Beau Soleil made house calls. He enjoyed house calls because they allowed him to be able to see patients in their own homes, to see how they lived, who lived with them, how the family seemed to function or not function, and how happy they seemed to be. If he knew the family, he could care better for the patient. His one problem with making house calls was that he could not afford a good horse. He was able to buy an old plow horse named Lucky who by now had outlived his name; he should have been renamed Methuselah at this time in his long life, and Beau often referred to him by that name. Lucky was ancient and barely got Dr. Soleil to his appointed rounds. Consequently, Beau walked when he could. He went through two pairs of shoes the first months he was in practice.

ONE LATE EVENING ON a cold November night, just a few months after their return to Sure Hope, Beau was asleep with Grace in their cottage. Grace by now was eight months into her pregnancy. Beau was awakened by a loud and insistent knock on the door. *Knock, Knock, Knock!!*

Wolf's ears pricked up, the fur on his back stood erect, and he began to snarl and bark. Beau roused himself, rolled out of bed, and shivered. He tried to be quiet and attempted to calm Wolf so as not to awaken Grace. Too late. Grace had heard the knocking. And the barking. Because of her pregnancy, Grace had not been sleeping well for the past month and she awakened easily.

It was winter in the mountains and the floor was cold. It creaked as Beau stepped toward the front door. He patted

Wolf on the head and whispered, "It's alright, boy." Beau opened the door and a blast of icy wind sliced through his thin nightshirt. There stood a young, lanky, tall, rawboned man in a papery shirt and ragged coat. He was obviously cold and frightened; his eyes were wide and he spoke in a hurried cadence. He was shivering. By his unkempt and dirty appearance, scraggly beard, and manner of speaking, it was apparent he was from the other side of the mountain. It was also apparent that he was poor.

"Doctor, my wife is having a baby and she is doing poorly. Please come and help her!" The stranger spoke in the strange mountain dialect that revealed remnants of its origins in the Tidewater area of Virginia. Beau recognized the accent. The man's family had arrived in the mountains many years before, having migrated from Princess Anne County. The courtly, genteel speech of the man seemed a strange contradiction to his appearance. Beau noticed the telltale signs of the Tidewater accent: out was pronounced *oat*, house came out *hoase,* and about became *aboat.*

It never occurred to Dr. Soleil to ask how he was going to be paid. He said, "Come in and warm yourself. Sit by the fire. Let me get my clothes on and I'll be right with you." Beau dressed hurriedly, put on his coat and gloves, grabbed his medical bag, and ran to the front door. He kissed Grace goodbye and went outside with the man.

As the two men left the house, Beau saw that the

visitor had ridden one horse and brought along another. With a motion of his hand, the stranger said, "Dr. Soleil, I've heard about Methuselah. I brought you one of my horses to ride. Please get on and follow me." Beau wondered how the man had heard about Lucky, but he was glad he had brought another horse. The distance to the man's home would have been too far and the incline too steep for the old horse. The stranger gathered his reins in his cold, ungloved hands, and urged his horse to carry him as fast as he could. Beau followed. The young man said his name was Charles Powers.

They ascended with all possible speed to the mountain pass and made it through to the other side. It was snowing by then, and both men were chilled to the core thirty minutes later when they arrived at the rude log cabin that was the Powers home, located near Fredericks' Draft. They rapidly dismounted and entered the front door. Beau noticed there was a plume of smoke from the chimney, and was glad for the hope of warming his cold, numb fingers; he could not help anyone with his fingers and hands in this condition. He went to the pretty, young, laboring mother and his heart melted. Beau had a tender heart, and he was deeply moved by women and children in need. Liza Powers had been in labor for a day and a half, and she was exhausted. It was clear that she was a petite woman, obvious even with her lying in bed. Surrounding her were her mother, her mother-in-law, and now Charles. On the floor were enough blood and blood-soaked cloths to make Beau fearful that something was very wrong.

"Jesus, help us," he prayed silently.

Liza was drenched in perspiration; she was moaning, she was pale, and she was suffering. Dr. Soleil asked her how she felt, and she merely nodded at him, her eyes half-closed, her hair matted on her forehead with sweat. He removed his pocket-watch from his vest and checked her pulse: it was 155 and thready. She had lost too much blood. He worried that she was dying.

Beau Soleil knew what he must do. He asked for clean water and soap, washed his hands, warmed them near the fire, and then opened his bag. From it he pulled several sets of forceps. He was happy to have been trained in Philadelphia in the expert use of forceps. (He was also thankful to the ingenuity of the Peter Chamberlen family for having invented and developed obstetrical forceps. As Huguenots, they had fled religious persecution in France and had become obstetricians to the royal family of England.) He examined the young mother, gave her something for pain, and then, using all the skill he had acquired in training, manipulated the forceps to close around the baby's head. He rotated the head, and then pulled out a red-headed boy. The infant boy was floppy, blue, and not breathing. He vigorously stimulated the little boy, praying to God to save his life, Beau's heart dying as he waited to see what would happen. There was a feeble cry, then a great wail. Everyone laughed and cried. A new baby boy was born, and he was fine! His color became a bright pink as he cried, now loudly. He squalled, he kicked, and he was fine. Now, his red hair was the only thing brighter than his red body. Liza sank back in relief; she was utterly spent. Charles Powers excitedly took the young doctor's hand in both of his large, calloused, bony hands and almost shook his arm off. It was 11:59 p.m., just one minute before midnight.

Relieved, Dr. Soleil turned and re-examined his patient, and now *he* became pale. No. This could not be. There was another baby, and this one was breech, coming feet-first. "Oh, no," he thought, "a double-footling breech!" This could be the death of Liza and the baby. The baby was not going to come down by itself. "Dear God, please help me, and help Liza and this baby!" Beau cried in his heart. He was terrified. How can I explain the terror that besieges a doctor in the early morning when he is alone and when there is nothing to do for a patient near death except what he can do, trusting God to do something great? It is a feeling of fear, aloneness, helplessness, and desperation. It is a feeling that the patient's life depends upon him, and the massive weight of responsibility is crushing and horrifying. Beau summoned all his courage and training, then carefully pulled the baby's legs out. He pulled some more to get the baby's body out. He then applied a different set of forceps to pull the baby's head down and out. Slowly, steadily, powerfully, he pulled. The head began to descend. Then, very cautiously, he pulled the head out, his fingers in the baby's mouth for leverage. The child was born at 12:32 a.m. Another boy!

But the trauma of birth had extracted its toll. This little boy was not crying, and he was not even breathing. He was as limp as a rag doll. Beau felt his umbilical cord for a pulse: he could feel a weak and very slow pulse. This baby would be dead if he did not act. He wiped off the baby's face, then placed his own mouth over the baby's mouth and nose. He slowly and gently blew into the baby's lungs so that he could see his chest rise. After several breaths, the baby began to move. Beau gave two more breaths, and then the baby got mad. The infant began to squall and scream. His color became more pink. His heart rate climbed. He was saved! There were two Powers boys, born with different birthdays, and they were both alive. Alive! The second baby had dark, black hair, and an olive complexion. Both boys were vigorous, both were hungry (a foretaste of the future), and both were well.

"Thank God!" exclaimed Liza's mother.

"Yes," Beau replied, "thank God."

It was too much for the new father, Charles Powers.

Beau looked around to congratulate him, and he was face down on the floor. He had passed out. Beau went to this new patient and gently rolled him over on his side, roused him, and had them bring him something to drink and eat. He survived.

The twin sons were quickly placed to Liza's breasts and they nursed surprisingly well, as if they knew what they were doing. Liza glowed with joy, and was more beautiful now than at any time in her life. A new mother radiates an almost inexpressible glory and beauty, unconsciously but truly, and it is enough to make a man draw back in wonder, awe, and reverence. She was utterly weary, and she drifted off to a peaceful sleep. The boys slept like—well, like babies, and Charles looked like a man who had just been through a war, only the life at stake had not been his own, but the lives of his three most precious possessions.

Dr. Beau Soleil collapsed in a ladder-back chair in the corner of the cabin, not far from the fire. He slouched in the chair, his clothes askew, blood all over his sweat-soaked shirt. His sleeves were still rolled up, and he could barely move. He was tired, but it was a good tired. He was not sleepy—yet. He was not even hungry. He had just given his all, and God had blessed him. He was grateful. He was spent.

By 5:00 a.m. it had stopped snowing, but the snow had covered the mountains in the darkness. Beau now dozed in the corner chair, his head nodding often and jerking him awake. He checked in on his three patients every thirty minutes or so, and they were all doing well. At about six o'clock, Liza's mother, Jessica, began fixing breakfast, and Beau finally left his chair to face the day. His legs ached and could barely carry him; they always felt weak after an all-nighter like this. Jessica offered him some breakfast and coffee. He eagerly sipped the coffee, dark and black without milk or sugar; he hated ruining a good cup of black coffee. He needed to feel the bite and jolt of strong coffee each morning. He was ravenous now, and ate the eggs and cornbread Jessica had prepared. The eggs were fried on an old, black, iron skillet. The yolks were unbroken. The cornbread was crispy and sweet, made with love. It helped him to regain his strength.

They discussed the babies and Beau asked Charles, "What are their names?"

Without hesitation, Charles calmly replied, "James and John."

"Those are wonderful names. Why James and John?"

"Because they are my sons of thunder."

"I don't understand. Why sons of thunder?"

"Because on a night when they were only a distant and far-off hope, there was thunder and lightning on the mountain like I have never seen. It rained in great sheets, the thunder rattled our cabin, and the lightning lit up the earth and sky. It lasted for hours. And I love James and John, the brothers that followed Jesus. They loved Jesus, and they loved him with a passion. Jesus called them the sons of thunder. They shook the world for the Kingdom of God. I want my two sons to love Jesus and to do something great for him and his Kingdom. They are James and John. Sons of thunder."

Beau thoughtfully stroked his beard. "Hmm, James and John. Sons of thunder. Beautiful names. Especially for twin boys."

After one final check on Liza, James, and John, Beau gave instructions to both of the new parents. He told them he would return later that day to check on them.

Charles offered a horse to Beau for the trip home and the return trip. As he mounted, they shook hands again. Charles had tears in his eyes. He thanked Beau for saving his family. Beau told him that God, not he, had saved his family. Charles then said, "Doc, I don't have much money. I'm a poor farmer but I raise horses—they are the best horses in the state. Please let me pay you with what I have. I have a two-year-old colt who will be ready to ride soon. He'll be a stallion one day. Would you allow me to pay you with the colt? You can have him in *aboat* three or four months." Dr. Beau Soleil told him it was too much, and that he needed the horse himself for his own family. Charles insisted. Finally, Beau agreed that in the spring, he would accept the colt. He thanked him.

Beau left Fredericks' Draft and rode down into town. The sun was rising over the mountains, giving life to the snow, which now appeared to be millions of unique, perfectly cut, glistening diamonds covering the mountains and hills. Beau thanked God for the beauty of his creation, and for being his refuge and strength, a very present help in time of trouble. "Thank you, God," he repeated over and over as he looked toward heaven. "Thank you."

Beau Soleil had a new horse. He would call him Thunder.

15

OLD JEFF

OLD JEFF lived alone.

Jefferson Peregrine Walker lived by himself and with himself. He lived in an old run-down cabin five miles or so from Sure Hope. His home was really a shack. He had little contact with others and kept to himself most of the time. He had a small plot of land and fed himself from a garden that he planted every spring and from hunting in the woods around his home. Jeff Walker was usually unshaven and unwashed. He spent most days in bed sleeping or in a chair sitting in a semiconscious state.

Occasionally Jeff came to town to buy a few supplies, but these visits were rare and often unpleasant. When he walked into town, wearing old, dirty, tattered clothes, smelling like he had not bathed for months (which was often the case), sporting a ragged beard, and covering his greasy, gray, longish hair with an old U.S. Army cap, people scattered. But the most remarkable thing about him was that his right trouser leg was empty and he walked with crutches. Adults avoided him; hypocritically, they whispered to each other about him after a chance encounter with him in which they gave him a smiling, fake "howdy"—as if they cared. Little boys mocked him and laughed at him. "Here comes Old Jeff!" they cried.

Jefferson Peregrine Walker was a lonely and sad old man.

Jefferson Peregrine Walker was an opium addict.

FROM EARLIEST MEMORY, Beau Soleil had heard of Old Jeff Walker but had only rarely seen him and had never spoken to him. Their paths never crossed. They never crossed, that is, until Old Jeff needed a physician. On that January day in 1891, Beau Soleil met Jefferson Peregrine Walker face to face.

A neighbor of Beau's heard from a friend that Jeff Walker was severely ill or maybe dying. Jeff was truly old now. Someone had passed his home and seen Jeff leaning over his fence rail. He seemed to be struggling to get back to his cabin. The passerby stopped and helped Jeff back inside. He seemed weak and barely coherent. The neighbor left a note for Beau at his home, and Beau felt it his duty to go to Jeff's cabin to offer his assistance.

Beau finished seeing his last patient of the day and rode to Jeff's homestead. It was cold but not snowing. The fences surrounding Jeff's home had tumbled down and the wood was rotten. Beau wended his way through the debris of the yard and was greeted by two ugly, barking dogs. Beau talked quietly and softly to the dogs as he slowly walked to the door, never turning his back on them. The dogs snarled and growled but never came near him. Beau was glad he had left Wolf at home.

He knocked on the door until he heard someone murmur the words, "Come in."

Beau pushed open the door and saw a thin, gaunt man crumpled in a chair near the fireless fireplace. He appeared to be about seventy, but it was hard to tell for sure in the darkening room. It was cold in the cabin and the man was shivering, draped in a filthy, tattered old blanket. He looked at Beau with half-closed eyes. His sallow skin was dirty and he was completely unkempt. He nodded at Beau and motioned for him to come closer.

The smell inside the cabin was sickening. It was putrid. It was cloacal.

Beau introduced himself. "Mr. Walker, I'm Beau Soleil. I'm a doctor from Sure Hope. I've heard you're not feeling well, and I've come to help if I can."

Jeff again nodded. He was breathing irregularly.

Beau gently removed Jeff's old blanket and wrapped him in a new wool blanket he had brought with him from home. He then began to build a fire, all the while observing

Jeff. As soon as the kindling was ablaze, Beau found a chair that was not broken and pulled it to Jeff's side. He sat down and withdrew from his satchel some hot soup that Grace had made and poured it into a tin cup for Jeff. He began to spoon it into Jeff's mouth and gave him sips of water between the spoonfuls of soup. Beau added logs to the blazing fire.

It appeared that Jeff was reviving. After about thirty minutes, he spoke.

"Dr. Soleil, thank you for coming. I am sick but I don't think you can help me. I'm dying. My body is wearing out. My mind is weak. My soul is sick." Jeff spoke in short, staccato sentences between labored breaths. His face was strained and perspiring. He continued to shiver.

"Mr. Walker, are you still cold?" was Beau's worried response.

"I am freezing, Doc." Jeff could barely squeeze the words out.

Beau sat Jeff up in the chair and he pulled him closer to the hearth. A little later, Jeff seemed to be improving so Beau asked him about himself. Beau wanted to and needed to understand what was wrong with Jeff Walker.

And Jeff Walker began to talk.

"I was born in 1829 to good parents in Connecticut. My mother named me Jefferson Peregrine Walker. I was named after Thomas Jefferson. My middle name,

Peregrine, is one my mother liked the sound of, but she never really knew what it meant. I learned later in life that it meant "wanderer" and I guess you could say that without realizing it, my mother named me well. My parents taught me the Bible and helped me to memorize Scripture. They were good parents. I joined the army when I was eighteen. I served under Robert E. Lee in the War with Mexico beginning in 1847. I managed to survive without any serious wounds. After the war, I settled in Texas."

Beau could tell from Jeff's increasing shortness of breath that he was laboring to talk. He tried to convince Jeff to rest for a while. Jeff stopped for a few minutes but then went on. He urgently, desperately needed to tell his story.

"I settled in Texas and married a wife. Her name was Susan. Susan was a lovely woman, the love of my life. Susan and I worked a farm in the Piney Woods of east Texas. Life was good for us. For a while. We had three children. But my family died of the fever in 1860. All except me. I stayed on to work the farm, but I was so downtrodden I could barely work. I had no heart for it. I had no purpose.

"The war started in 1861. I thought it would be all over soon, so I waited. It did not end quickly. I heard that General Lee had taken command of the Army of Northern Virginia and I went to join him because I respected him from the War with Mexico. Odd. My two brothers both fought for the North. I hope I never fought against them. I don't know if they are alive now or not."

Jeff stopped to rest again. Beau let him talk at his own pace. Beau knew that it was important for this man to tell about himself. He sensed that Jeff needed to unburden himself.

After a few minutes of silence, broken only by Jeff's raspy, shallow breathing and the popping of logs, Jeff resumed his tale. "When General Longstreet went to Chickamauga to reinforce General Bragg, I was sent there with him. It was 1863. The battle was fierce and deadly. I saw too many men on both sides die that day. I killed some myself; only God knows how many. I saw men shot through the head. I saw men blown up. I saw men run through with bayonets. I saw streams of blood coming down the hillside. I had bits of men's brains on my coat and blood on my cap and shirt. Men were screaming in agony all around me. They were crying. Men were dying. I still have nightmares about it.

"Our lieutenant had just commanded 'Fix bayonets!' I began charging Union troops when I noticed something round and black rolling quickly toward me. It was coming fast. Very fast. It seemed to be gaining speed. My mind told me what it was, but I could not react. I could not get out of the way. It was a cannon ball. It took my right leg off."

Here Jeff began to sob. "Doctor, it took my right leg off. From the knee down."

Jeff stopped to catch his breath. His tears flowed and he was not ashamed. He spoke again.

"We won the battle but I lost my leg." His voice weakened and he stopped speaking.

Beau listened and felt compassion for this old man. He was beginning to understand him.

Jeff Walker continued. "A friend saw me go down. He used his belt as a tourniquet to stop the bleeding. They took me to the surgical tent. The surgeon rushed to my side and after a glance, realized that my lower leg was missing and my upper leg was shattered. He gave me a shot of morphine to ease the pain. He closed the wound the best he could. But within three days I had developed gangrene."

Jeff paused again, then resumed his story. "The doctor came to my cot and spoke gently to me. 'You have developed gangrene. It will kill you if we don't act now. We have to take your leg off at the mid-thigh to save your life.' I told him to just let me die. I thought to myself, 'What good is a man with one leg?' He gave me no choice. Within a few minutes, they gave me some brandy. As they prepared for the operation, I saw the knife, the saw, and the bandages. They soaked a napkin in chloroform, shaped it into a cone, and then placed it over my face. They waited for me to pass out, and they did the amputation.

"A few days later, I was placed in a rail car and transferred to Augusta, Georgia. The Presbyterian church there had been converted into a hospital for wounded soldiers. Curious—the church yard had also become a holding place for Union prisoners.

"My leg was no longer there but I still had bad pain. It was like my leg was gone but I could still feel the cannon ball taking it off. All the time. Every day. I think they call it phantom pain. Or ghost pain. They gave me shots of morphine and opium pills to dull the pain. And the more they gave me, the more I needed it.

"Doctor, I did not want to live. I could not bear the memories of the grisly battles. I could not bear to live by myself with one leg. I could not bear the loss of my family anymore. And I could not bear to live without opium."

Short of breath, Jeff stopped talking again. But he needed to tell his story. With gathered strength, he went on.

"In the church hospital, a gentle young doctor, a Dr. Joseph Jones, came by to see me often. He told me not to lose hope. He tried to encourage me. He told me that Jesus loves me. I could not believe it. I wanted to believe it. But I felt so unworthy. I felt guilty and ashamed. I had lost all respect for myself. I had lost all hope. I had one leg. I was useless. I now depended on a drug to get me through my days. I thought that my manhood and my morality had vanished. How could Jesus love a man like me? How could anyone love a man like me?

"I'm sorry to say that I survived. Death was better than

life to me. The war ended and I drifted all over the South. I drifted to any town where I could get some morphine or opium. I finally settled in Sure Hope in 1868. Why? I don't know. I just landed here. I found a cabin and land I could buy, away from people. I found ways to get opium to dull my pain. I cannot live without it.

"Now I'm dying."

Jeff's face was pale now and dripping with sweat and tears. He shivered more, not from the cold, but from chills and fever. Then he drew aside the blankets and pulled up his right pants leg to show his doctor. The sickening odor in the room increased and became almost unbearable. Beau saw that the trousers were stiff with dried drainage and blood; thick liquid, putrid pus, was dripping to the floor. Beau knew then that Jeff was suffering from osteomyelitis. It was a chronic bone infection that had begun many years ago. Jeff was now dying of infection—sepsis. His death was very near.

Jeff wanted to talk some more. "Doctor, I have lived with shame and guilt and fear for many years. I'm ashamed of my amputation. I'm ashamed and feel guilty that I need opium to live. I need the opium to deaden my pain and to deaden my mind. I'm addicted to opium. I cannot help myself. I didn't mean to get addicted; they gave it to me for pain. I feel guilty that I've killed people in battle. I feel guilty that I'm alive and my friends are dead. I feel guilty that I could not stop my family from dying. I am afraid of what people say and think about me. And I'm afraid to die. I'm terrified to meet God. Do you think Jesus can possibly love someone like me?"

Beau again realized that God had not called him to be only a physician of the body, as noble as that is: God had called him to be a physician of the soul also. In front of him was a man desperately in need of soul healing.

Gently, tenderly, earnestly, Beau replied to Jeff. "Mr. Walker, God loves you. He sees your suffering and your pain. He sent his Son, Jesus, to die for suffering sinners like you and me—sinners who are guilty and ashamed and afraid. Every human I know is full of shame, guilt, and fear. Each of us needs forgiveness. Each of us needs redemption. Jesus looks on us with mercy and love. Jesus looks on *you* with mercy and love. Each of us needs the love of Jesus. No one needs Jesus more and no one needs him less. Don't look at yourself. Look away from yourself. Look at your Savior, nailed to the cross as he suffered, bled, and died for your sins. And look at your Savior, no longer on the cross; he is now the risen Lord and King. He will have mercy on you. He loves you. He has had mercy on me."

Jeff Walker closed his eyes. His grimaces revealed his suffering. The sweats and shivering continued. He could not get warm, even with the blanket and the roaring fire. Jeff opened his eyes once again, just briefly, gathering all his strength with a supreme act of the will. With raspy voice, he whispered, "Lord Jesus Christ, Son of God, have mercy on me, a sinner." He closed his eyes and slumped back in his chair for a few seconds. Then he mumbled a few words. He repeated them. Twice. Three times. The words were barely audible and Beau could not understand them. Beau leaned over him and put his ear near Jeff's mouth. He listened carefully and was finally able to decipher Jeff's words: "Today, thou shalt be with me in paradise."

Jeff's breathing slowed and stopped.

He was finally at peace.

And the peregrinations of Jefferson Peregrine Walker ended with his going home to rest—forever.

16

RESURRECTION

LIFE RACED FORWARD FOR Beau Soleil and his young family. The days and years quickly, silently, almost imperceptibly flew by. It was now 1898 and Beau was thirty-three years old. He had been back home in Sure Hope for almost nine years. He had cared for thousands of patients.

ON A CHILLY APRIL morning, just as Beau finished breakfast, a rider stormed into view.

It was early springtime in the mountains. Fragrant aromas of mountain grass and mountain flowers, sights of dogwoods and redbuds in bloom and the unique soft-green new growth of trees in spring, the feel of the cool of the morning as the sun begins to rise—all these combined to make Beau appreciate creation and its Creator. Truly, he thought to himself, the mercies of the Lord are new every morning.

Beau had been sitting on the front porch, reading his Bible and praying, readying himself for the day ahead and reviewing events of the night before. He was still pondering the previous night as he enjoyed his breakfast.

Beau's dream had recurred the night before. In it, through gray-blue tones, he saw a pale, slender woman wandering slowly and aimlessly in the snow on a cold night. The woman was carrying a bundle. As always, Beau never saw her face but somehow he knew she was sad. He never saw what the bundle contained. The experience was so real that it terrified and depressed him. Grace was awakened by his hard breathing and agitated mumbling. She gently shook him awake and as she did, she felt the cold sweat drenching his nightshirt.

"Beau, you're dreaming again. Wake up. It's all a dream. It is alright." She hugged him close to herself and spoke calming words to him.

"Grace, this same dream keeps coming back. I do not know why. I don't know what it means, if anything. But it terrifies me and I can't understand why, or where it comes from, or where it is going." Beau's distress eventually gave way to peace. He changed his nightshirt and returned to bed.

Neither Beau nor Grace slept well that night.

BEAU'S BREAKFAST REVERIE WAS interrupted by sudden hoofbeats. Wolf was on the porch with Beau and seemed agitated before Beau heard or saw anything. Wolf was on his feet, alert and pacing. He growled and barked, and his ears stood upright. Beau looked up to see a rider galloping from the woods. The horseman was on a black stallion. It was clear that he had ridden for hours; the horse was in a lather and the rider was mud-spattered. It was also clear he was on an urgent mission.

The rider dismounted and from his right breast pocket he withdrew a note that he handed Beau. Beau quickly observed that this was no ordinary man. He appeared to be about twenty-five years old and he was massive. He was about 6'5" and weighed at least 250 pounds. He was thickly muscled and his large hands could crush a man's skull.

The man did not speak. Beau quickly realized he *could* not speak. He could not hear. He made signs to Beau to read the note.

The letter was written in an elegant, almost feminine hand, black ink on white paper, and contained an urgent request:

Dear Dr. Soleil,

My name is Michael Fletcher. I live on the other side of the mountain with my older sister. My sister is very ill and needs a doctor. She can't breathe. It is an emergency.

*Can you please come now? Follow me and I'll take you
to her.*

Beau knew he must go. Despite the mystery and the
sudden surprise, he knew in his heart he must go. He
pulled a pencil from his pocket and wrote on the back
of the note, "I will follow you in a few minutes. Let me
gather a few things." Beau handed the note to the man,
who acknowledged that he understood. He turned to go
inside and showed the man's note to Grace, gentle and wise
Grace. He explained the situation to her, incomplete as his
knowledge was. She immediately said, "Beau, you need
to go."

Beau rapidly retrieved his coat and hat, gathered
together all he needed in his medical bag, grabbed two
biscuits and some water, and then mounted his stallion
Thunder. Beau loved this horse. Wolf was at their side; he
would not leave his master.

Beau followed Michael through town and then forded
the Shenandoah River, heading westward. For three hours
they went west, over hills, then over a mountain, following
steep switch-back trails. At about eleven o'clock, they
arrived at a small three-room house just on the other side of
the mountain. The house faced a small valley, rich and lush
with the coming of spring. Smoke rose from the chimney,
a fire still being needed to take the chill out of the house.

Dr. Soleil and Michael dismounted and Michael led

the way into the home. The house was clean and well-kept. A low fire was burning in the fireplace. Beau saw two small bedrooms, one to each side of the main room. The main room was simply furnished with table and chairs. The kitchen was in a corner of the room. In the opposite corner was a small table with a few framed daguerreotypes; Beau assumed these were family members.

Just to the side of the fireplace was a small, slight woman lying in a makeshift bed, propped up by three pillows. She seemed to be in her fifties. She greeted Beau with a shy, weary smile and the words, "Thank you for coming, Dr. Soleil." It was all she could say. She was short of breath and the words came between pants for air.

Beau went to her gently and kindly took her hand. He introduced himself, softly saying, "Miss Fletcher, I'm Beau Soleil. I came as soon as Michael handed me the note. I hope to be able to help you. Can you please explain to me what is wrong?"

As he spoke and held her hand, he imperceptibly moved his fingers to her wrist and was surprised to find her pulse was extremely rapid.

Christina Fletcher spoke slowly and with difficulty. She had to take breaths between her words and could not finish a complete sentence without stopping to breathe. "For about the last year or so, I have had difficulty breathing. I have had trouble working and have had to rest frequently.

Now, I can't work much at all. I have no energy. At night, I must sleep propped with pillows. I cannot lie flat. I've gotten a lot worse in the past day."

Beau Soleil listened patiently and attentively. He felt compassion for this woman.

"Please allow me to examine you, Miss Fletcher."

She nodded her assent and he proceeded to take her pulse again, to listen to her heart and lungs with his stethoscope, and to feel her abdomen. He looked at her legs.

He found her heart to be racing at 140 beats per minute, regular but rapid. Her neck veins were distended. Her lungs had crackles, her heart had a loud murmur and gallop, and her liver was enlarged. Her legs were swollen over her shins, her feet were swollen in the same way, and he could press his finger into the soft swelling and cause pitting.

The diagnosis was clear. Christina Fletcher was suffering from decompensated congestive heart failure. Beau removed his stethoscope from his ears and began to explain his findings.

"Miss Fletcher, I know what your problem is and I think I can help you." Beau chose his next words carefully. He spoke softly and in a way that would not cause her to be afraid. "You are short of breath because you are in heart failure. I have some medicine I want you to take that will make you feel better. I think you will be up on your feet within a week."

Christina looked at him appreciatively, unable to talk further.

Beau continued as he withdrew a vial of medication from his black bag. "Here is some digitalis. I want you to take six drops twice per day. Also, you should decrease your salt intake drastically. No added salt, no high salt foods. No ham. No bacon. I think you will be better in a few days. You will notice that you are breathing easier, that you are less swollen, and that you will have more energy."

Beau paused for a few moments to allow Christina to absorb what he had said.

He resumed his comments. "I'll return in two days to check on you. And I will leave written instructions for both you and Michael."

"Thank you, Doctor," she whispered.

He turned to Michael and motioned for him to come over to him. He then wrote out instructions for Michael and Christina. At the end of the note, he wrote, "Michael, do you understand? Do you have any questions?"

Michael grasped the pen and wrote, "No questions, Doctor. Thank you." Michael demonstrated the same elegant script as before.

Before he left, Beau looked into Christina's face and told her she would be fine. He told her he would pray for her, and then bowed his head to pray for her right there.

Tears filled Christina's soft blue eyes. She reached for the young doctor's hand with a soft, "Thank you. Thank you."

Michael's moist eyes revealed both gratitude and love.

As Beau turned to leave, he silently thanked God for allowing him to care for this poor woman, and for giving him the wisdom to know what to do. And he had the fleeting thought that this brother and sister bore little resemblance to each other. He wondered if it meant anything.

BEAU RETURNED TWO DAYS later, as promised. It was Good Friday. The weather was warm and sunny as he departed. At noon, halfway to the Fletchers' home, the sky darkened and a light rain began to fall. It continued to rain until he arrived at their home.

Beau enjoyed rain. He always had. He enjoyed seeing it from inside a warm, dry home. He enjoyed being out in it. He delighted in the smell of rain, especially in the spring as it penetrated the earth below. He did not mind getting wet. A gentle rain produced for him an inner peace.

For about half an hour, the weather became ugly and menacing with fierce lightning and deafening thunder. The rain came down in columns of water and then finally slowed to a drizzle.

Of course, it took longer than usual to traverse the muddy mountain paths, but Thunder was sure-footed, and Beau arrived at the Fletchers' cabin safely, though wet and chilled. He was happy to see smoke rising from the chimney. Michael showed him inside. It was immediately clear to Beau that Christina was better: she was standing in the kitchen. Beau entered their home, hung up his coat and hat, and went straight to the fireside to get warm and dry. He chatted with the Fletchers as he warmed himself. He observed Christina as they talked. Her breathing seemed normal now.

"Doctor, God has healed me! And he has used you to do it! Thank you!" Christina was full of joy and excitement. Michael seemed happy and unafraid as well. He stood nearby, as always, waiting to be of any assistance. He loved his sister.

"I am so glad, Miss Fletcher. You look even better today than I was hoping for."

"Please call me Christina, Doctor. Everyone calls me that."

"Then I will call you Christina." Beau was warm by now and continued. "If you don't mind, please allow me to examine you again. Maybe we should go to your bedroom for the exam?"

The makeshift bed by the fireplace was no longer present. Christina, Micheal, and Beau all made their way into Christina's bedroom. Beau watched Christina as she walked to the bedroom and noted no signs of breathing difficulty. He pulled a chair to her bedside and asked her to sit on the edge of the bed.

"Are you sleeping better? Is your energy improved?" Beau asked the questions casually but her answers were keys to his assessment.

"Yes," said his patient in a clear and unlabored voice. "I have my energy back again, and I slept flat last night for the first time in weeks."

Beau took Christina's pulse and found it to be about ninety. Her lungs were clear. He asked her to lie down. Her heart's gallop had disappeared. Her murmur was decreased. Her liver edge was normal. The leg swelling was almost gone.

Beau announced to both Christina and Michael that she was indeed much better. The doctor was pleased with his patient's progress.

It was about 2:00 p.m. and the rain was still falling. Christina asked if Beau would stay for some coffee. He accepted the offer, and within a few minutes, Beau, Christina, and Michael were seated together at the table. Their conversation was pleasant and light. Michael smiled and nodded, happy to see his sister improving. The coffee was just what Beau needed. He knew he must leave soon to see other patients. Besides, Beau could tell that Christina was tiring. He determined not to stay long.

"Christina, you have made remarkable progress. I need to leave but I will come back in three or four days to check on you again. If you need me before then, send Michael."

He realized that Michael understood much of what he was saying. It was obvious to Beau that over the years, Michael had become adept at reading lips and other social cues. Beau smiled and addressed Michael directly.

"Michael, your sister is better. I will return in several days. Come for me if you need me sooner."

Michael smiled and nodded that he understood.

A FEW DAYS PASSED and Beau again made plans to return to the other side of the mountain to pay a visit to the Fletchers. He looked forward to this house call. He enjoyed being with the Fletchers. He expected even more improvement in Christina's condition. He anticipated the joy and gratification he would feel. It is a high privilege to be an instrument of healing.

On April 12, 1898, Beau made the trek to the Fletchers' again. Easter Sunday had just occurred two days before and, in his heart, Beau was still celebrating the resurrection of Jesus Christ. "He is risen. He is risen indeed. Alleluia!" The words kept coming back to his mind as he rode over the mountain. Beau exulted as he rode, enjoying the mountain springtime in all its glory. Spring spoke to him yet again of the resurrection of Christ: life after death, light after darkness, hope after despair, joy after sadness, the new replacing the old, glorious beauty from monotone gray.

Upon his arrival, Michael showed him in. Christina was up, working, singing, and happy.

"Oh, Dr. Soleil, I feel wonderful! Thank you for coming again."

"Christina, do you feel normal again?"

"Yes, oh yes! I have not felt so fine for months."

Beau quickly examined her, and her exam, except for her heart murmur, was completely normal now. Her heart rate was eighty and regular. Her lungs were clear and there was no swelling of her legs. He told Christina and Michael that she was doing well, extremely well. He would continue to treat her with the digitalis and would return in a month, or, if they made a trip to Sure Hope in the next few weeks, he would see her in town.

Glad of Christina's recovery and knowing that he had many other patients to see, Beau rose to leave.

Christina, however, wanted to talk. She implored Beau to stay for a few minutes. She had baked some cookies and Beau could not resist the offer. They all sat down to enjoy the freshly-baked sweets and some coffee.

Christina began the conversation. "Dr. Soleil, you may wonder about our family. Michael is twenty-nine years old now and was born after I was adopted by our parents. Both our father and mother died a few years ago. They were wonderful people who loved God with their whole hearts, and because of that, they loved everyone. In the 1850s and 1860s, our parents were part of the Underground Railroad. They were stationmasters, and this house was a station along the way for slaves escaping to freedom to the northern states and Canada. More than one hundred slaves passed through here. Our parents hid them, protected them, sheltered them, aided them, clothed them, and fed them."

Beau's mind went immediately to his Philadelphia friend, George Smith. "Surely," Beau thought, "this must be the station George passed through on his way to freedom!" Without speaking or interrupting, he waited for Christina to continue.

Christina took a sip of coffee and then went on with her account. "Michael was a healthy child until he developed a serious brain infection when he was nine months old. He had high fever for about a week and developed seizures. He had a strange stiffness of the neck, so much that he held his head tilted backwards for a month or so. He recovered— except for the fact that he could not hear afterwards. He is completely deaf and because of that, he never learned to talk. He is good at reading lips. He is smart. I taught him to write. He has a beautiful handwriting.

"I cared for Michael during his illness and later. I became a second mother to him. He loves me and would do anything for me. I depend upon him for protection. He is a gentle soul. However, if anyone ever tried to harm me, Michael would not be merciful."

She sipped her coffee again and leaned back. For a brief interval, no one said a word.

Birds were singing outside the Fletcher home. The only other sounds were the occasional creaking of chairs and the clinking of cups and saucers.

Beau listened to Christina's story attentively, patiently, and silently. It seemed to him that Christina was answering unspoken questions and removing shrouds from mysteries. He was eager to learn more. By now, he had lost interest in the cookies. Beau waited for Christina to continue.

She smiled, shifted in her chair, and resumed her narrative. "As for me—how did I come to be adopted? There is much I do not know. My father was out in the cold winter night of Christmas Eve, 1864. He was searching for slaves that were escaping to his house for shelter, rest, and warmth. They were late, and he was concerned they had become lost in the snowstorm. He came near Sure Hope and finally found them, three poorly clad black men, shivering and frightened. My father wrapped them in warm blankets, gave them some bread and bacon to eat, and had them pile into his hay wagon, hiding in the back.

"He carried them back over the mountain and just as the sun arose on Christmas morning, only a mile or so from our home, they found a young girl who had collapsed in a snowdrift. She was unconscious and was barely breathing. Her lips were blue. Her thin cotton dress was soaked and did little to protect her from the fierce cold. She had not frozen—yet.

"My father placed her in the back of the wagon with the escaped slaves and wrapped her in the remaining blankets.

"Doctor, I was that girl. For the next few days, my very life was in doubt. I was in and out of consciousness. I remember nothing about it. My mother undressed me, warmed me, bathed me, dressed me in her own warm clothes, fed me hot soup, gave me water to drink, and nursed me back to consciousness. When I was fully awake, I did not know where I was. I did not know even *who* I was. I did not know my name. I still don't remember anything about my life before that day I awakened from my coma. Because my parents found me on Christmas Day, they gave me my name, Christina. They loved me and adopted me as their own daughter. And I have lived with this family ever since. When our parents died, Michael and I continued in the house together."

Like any good doctor, Beau thought. He asked a question. "Christina, please let me ask you so I'm clear. Please tell me again when you were discovered by your father. What year was it?"

"I have no memory of any of the events I just described.

But my parents told me they found me on December 25, 1864. Why do you ask?" Christina could not understand why Beau would take such an interest in her personal history.

Beau did not answer. His mind was present yet far away. As she recounted her story, Beau got up from the table and began pacing the room. As he paced and listened, he did what he always did as he thought: he reached into his left trousers pocket and fingered the brass button he always carried with him, rolling it and rubbing it and flipping it. The button, as always, somehow calmed him and increased his ability to think. Christina's story was unusual. He remembered having read about patients who had entered a fugue state after some traumatic experience. In this state, from the moment of trauma, some patients lost any memory of prior events and even of their own identity. Could this be what had happened to her?

Still rolling and manipulating the brass button, still pacing, he walked over to the table in the corner of the room and studied the pictures. He assumed these were Mr. and Mrs. Fletcher. They were a handsome pair. He also noticed something near one of the pictures that seemed oddly out of place. It was a round metallic object. On closer inspection, it was a tarnished brass button. On the front of the button were the letters CSA.

"Christina, where did this button come from?" he asked quietly.

"My father found it in my hand when he rescued me from the snowdrift. Why?" Christina seemed perplexed.

Beau still played with the brass button in his pocket, rolling it between his thumb and fingers as he rolled Christina's story around in his mind.

"Christina, may I inspect the button?"

"Of course."

Beau picked up the button from the table and turned it over in his hands. He carefully examined it. He looked at the back and found the letters NW etched into the metal with the point of a knife.

He drew his own button from his pocket and compared the two. His own button was bright and shiny. The one on the table was dull and tarnished. But otherwise, they were identical. And the NW etched on the back was clearly done by the same hands and the same knife.

Beau was stunned.

He was silent.

He thought.

He knew.

He spoke.

"Christina, do you remember anything else about this button or about your life before you came here to live?"

"No, nothing at all."

"Let me show you something."

With that, Beau held his own shiny button in his left

hand and held the dull button in his right hand. He brought both buttons to Christina for her to see and compare.

She gasped.

It was immediately clear to her that the buttons were identical.

Suddenly Christina knew.

She knew everything. She knew who she was. She remembered her previous life. She remembered wandering in the snow—lost, grieving, and despairing on Christmas Eve and early Christmas Day. She remembered her infant son. She remembered her husband. Her memory was restored. She was released from her prison of amnesia.

And she wept.

She wept for her lost life. She wept for her lost son. She wept for her lost husband. And she wept for her healing and renewal.

Christina looked at Beau and through her tears whispered, "You look like your father."

At this, Beau's heart broke with sorrow, with joy, and with love.

Here, right in front of him, was his beloved mother who had suffered so much for him. Here was his mother, sick and in need of a physician, who in God's infinite wisdom and ordering of events, was now being treated by the son she had placed on a snowy doorstep so many years ago.

As tears tracked down his face, Beau softly said, almost inaudibly, almost involuntarily, "Thank you, God. Thank you, Mother."

And so the mother that had loved her son so much and with such desperation that she had entrusted him to others, now received him back to herself. She was restored, and her son was restored to her.

And Beau Soleil understood with new understanding that the love of God is the truest truth in the universe, permeating, suffusing, penetrating, undergirding, and controlling all of his creation. We see through a glass, darkly. Yet now Beau saw more clearly than ever the purpose of his life, the meaning of love, and the privilege of following Jesus Christ. Beau saw, with deeper clarity, that he had a sure and steadfast hope that anchored his soul to reality.

Beau felt the light, massive weight of the Psalmist's words as they welled over, unbidden, and flooded his mind and heart:

> *Surely goodness and mercy shall follow me*
> *all the days of my life,*
>
> *and I will dwell in the house of the Lord forever.*

It's all true," Beau thought. "It is all true."

Beau Soleil never had nightmares again.

He carried a brass button in his pocket until the day he died.

ॐॐॐ

… That by two immutable things, in which it was impossible for God to lie,

we might have a strong consolation,

who have fled for refuge to lay hold upon the hope set before us:

Which hope we have as an anchor of the soul, both sure and stedfast…

Hebrews 6:18-19a

ENDNOTES

1. Chapter 4. The part of this chapter about the gold coin in the bread is a story I heard as a child. I do not know who wrote the story, or if it is a part of a fairy tale. Because of that, I cannot give proper attribution.

2. Chapter 6, pages 80-82. Iain H. Murray, in his book, *Revival and Revivalism* (The Banner of Truth Trust, 1994, Carlisle, PA), succinctly and deftly describes The First Great Awakening and The Great Revival of Virginia. I am indebted to him for this background information.

3. Chapter 13, pages 183-185. In describing Mr. Pride, I credit three of my favorite authors for their influences. Beau's enjoyment of his dislike for Mr. Pride was inspired by Wendell Berry's *Jayber Crow*. The mayor's impressive bookshelf echoes a description from Ivo Andric's *The Bridge on the Drina*. And in Charles Dickens' *David Copperfield*, David wipes his hand off after shaking that of Uriah Heep.

4. Chapter 15, page 220. In *Cloud of Witnesses* (2004), David B. Calhoun writes the history of First Presbyterian Church, Augusta, Georgia. From pages 73-84, Dr. Calhoun gives an account of the church during the Civil War. I am thankful for his research and have used some specific facts from these pages as a part of Old Jeff's story.

5. Chapter 15. I found these websites helpful as I researched opiate addiction after the Civil War.

    https://library.medicine.yale.edu/blog/great-risk-opium-eating-how-civil-war-era-doctors-reacted-prescription-opioid-addiction

    https://www.smithsonianmag.com/history/inside-story-americas-19th-century-opiate-addiction-180967673/

    https://collections.nlm.nih.gov/bookviewer?PID=nlm:nlmuid-0257706-bk#page/76/mode/2up

6. Chapters 12, 13, 15, and 16. The Heidelberg Catechism, Question 1, both informs and amplifies much in these chapters.

    What is your only comfort in life and in death?

    That I am not my own, but belong—body and soul, in life and in death—to my faithful Savior, Jesus Christ.

    He has fully paid for all my sins with his precious blood, and has set me free from the tyranny of the devil.

    He also watches over me in such a way that not a hair can fall from my head without the will of my Father in heaven; in fact, all things must work together for my salvation.

    Because I belong to him, Christ, by his Holy Spirit, assures me of eternal life and makes me wholeheartedly willing and ready from now on to live for him.

ACKNOWLEDGMENTS

This book is the work of many years and I owe debts of gratitude to my family and friends for listening to my readings, for reviewing the multitude of updated manuscripts, for their incisive comments, and for their support.

To my wife Nancy: thank you for your patience. You have given me time alone with my endless writing, and have patiently and honestly read each new version. Your comments have been invaluable. You are my best critic. For better or worse, you know how I think.

To the rest of my family who endured reading and hearing a work in progress: thank you. My parents, my sister Becky Sandberg, my daughter Rebecca Weeks, and grandchildren Mary Weeks and Thomas Claassen gave me their advice and encouragement. Most of my grandchildren have heard some of these stories read to them; their reactions told me at least some of the content was good.

Friends George Hillman, Jessica Blanchard, Wayne Kerr, Tony Neal, and David Watkins read the manuscript at various stages and offered their insights and counsel, much of which is incorporated into this final version. Thank you.

Friend Jennifer Drake's eye for detail makes her both

a superlative pediatrician and book reviewer. Thank you, Jennifer, for your careful reading (twice) and for your suggestions.

Special thanks to friends Jeff and Pam Stovall for their support and encouragement.

Granddaughter Abby Weeks receives credit for the cover design. Thank you, Abby.

Thanks to Jim Bessey, my editor, who succeeded in understanding what I was attempting to do, and who gave me helpfully critical comments.

Thanks to Jose Ramirez at Pedernales Publishing for his always excellent assistance.

David Stacks of Stacks Editing gave me his valuable time and advice during the pre-publication phase. Thank you.

Thanks to you, dear reader, for entering the world of Sure Hope and Beau Soleil. I hope it was a satisfying and uplifting journey.

Finally, and most important, I am grateful to God for giving me this opportunity to write about the few things I know a little about: family, community, medicine, and, above all, sure hope in Christ.

Made in the USA
Columbia, SC
15 October 2022

69454304R00139